The Gregg Press
Science Fiction Series

Things to Come
by H. G. Wells

The Gregg Press Science Fiction Series

David G. Hartwell, *Editor*
L. W. Currey, *Associate Editor*

Things To Come

H. G. WELLS

With New Introductions by
ALLAN ASHERMAN
and
GEORGE ZEBROWSKI

SF-We
1975

c. 1

GREGG PRESS

A DIVISION OF G. K. HALL & CO., BOSTON, 1975

Printed on permanent/durable acid-free paper and bound in the United States of America.

Republished in 1975 by Gregg Press, A Division of G. K. Hall & Co., 70 Lincoln Street, Boston, Massachusetts 02111

Library of Congress Cataloging in Publication Data

Wells, Herbert George, 1866 - 1946.
   Things to come.

(The Gregg Press science fiction series)
A film story based on The shape of things to come.
Reprint of the ed. published by the Cresset Press, London.
   I. Wells, Herbert George, 1866 - 1946. The shape of things to come. II. Title.
PR5774.T45 1975   822'.9'12   75-11649
ISBN 0-8398-2318-5

Contents

Introduction by Allan Asherman   vii

Cast and Credits for the film *Things to Come*   xv

Scenes from the film *Things to Come*   xvii

Introduction by George Zebrowski   xxxiii

THINGS TO COME by H. G. Wells   1

Introduction

H.G. WELLS began his career as a combination historian and reporter, who used the irrevokable facts of yesterday to justify the happenings of his day. The wonder of this was that he didn't stop there, but used the current events of his time to extrapolate the future course of things. His book, *The Shape of Things to Come* (1933), was an exercise in this type of psycho-historical projection.

If only in the back of his mind, Wells probably intended *The Shape of Things to Come* to be the basis of a motion-picture. He was fascinated by films, even before they had attained sound. In 1929 he'd tried his hand at creating a finished screenplay, *The King Who Was a King* (mentioned briefly in his introductory notes here). Unfortunately, *The King Who Was a King* was structured around an open hostility to war; such an outlook was not in vogue at that time. The book was looked upon as an idealistic, cinematic experiment of Wells the eccentric genius and, along with some of the author's other eccentricities, was promptly forgotten. Even if there was interest in the vehicle, Wells' treatment would have been impossible to film. There were too many sets, locations, characters and vast scenes; it would have required an extraordinary producer, with a great deal of backing. There was none in Britain at that time, but there *was* one in the making.

Alexander Korda, the Hungarian-born producer, had tried his hand at filming in the United States. Discouraged with the American film industry, he took up residence in Great Britain, where he rapidly met with success. He managed to get backing, and set up a large studio at Elstree. His 1933 production, *The*

Private Life of Henry VIII, established his London Films as a
leader in the film industry and led to a partnership-distribution
agreement with United Artists.[1]

It was inevitable that Wells and Korda should get together, for
just as Wells was fascinated by film, Korda was stimulated by
solid writing. It was inevitable, too, that Korda would have to
"prune" Wells' genius to accommodate practical screen writing,
without watering down the author's style — a difficult project,
from both men's standpoints. If the author's notes in this volume
are any guide, Wells was content with the reworkings of his
writings and regarded them as refinements necessary for the
filming of *Things to Come.*

Director William Cameron Menzies had much to do with these
re-writes. Menzies, as much of a cinematic genius as Wells was a
literary one, had not been Korda's first choice to direct *Things to
Come.* The earliest press releases stated the film "One Hundred
Years to Come" would be directed by Lewis Milestone. It was
probably the offer to direct *Mutiny on the Bounty* that cancelled
his association with the project, leading Korda to send for Menzies. Responsible for the layout of Douglas Fairbanks' version of
The Thief of Bagdad, Menzies would later plan the visuals for
Korda's remake of the fantasy classic in 1940; in the same year
he would also work on Alfred Hitchcock's *Foreign Correspon-
dent.* His crowning achievement would be his designs for *Gone
with the Wind.* It was primarily Menzies' eye for vastness, combined with his practical understanding of what could be done
within certain budgets, that guided Wells' work. Sometimes
chided for his "stiff" direction of the people in *Things to Come,*
Menzies actually fulfilled Wells' wishes by treating the film's
characters as human symbols, rather than as individuals.

There were many changes along the way. Wells mentions the
existence of intermediate treatments, and we can only guess at
their contents. The script printed herein is represented as being
the "final" version, but it is still longer than the finished film,
and various scenes are treated somewhat differently than they
were filmed. Since the book was published in 1935, it's logical to
assume that at least one subsequent draft was done, and this
later draft is what the film follows.

There are two possible explanations for the scenes "missing"
altogether from the prints of *Things to Come* that survive today.
They might have appeared in the original British release print of
1936, but not the American version. Then, too, the film was
purchased by a re-issue distributor, Film Classics, in 1947. It
may have been re-issued in an aborted from, to save printing

costs. If this is so, these shortened prints are probably the ones available for viewing today. In either case, many of the "missing" scenes were actually filmed, as studio photographs were taken of many segments, both small and large, cut from surviving prints. Some of these stills accompany this introduction.

The short scene at the film's start, establishing the state of the world, was probably never included in the film, as the opening credits fade directly into the "Everytown" logo. The scene establishing young Harding working in his lab *was* shot, though not included in surviving prints.

The small sons of Cabal and Passworthy are not shown having their fight at the Christmas party. This is unfortunate as the sequence, when combined with little Horrie Passworthy's death, would immediately have established the self-perpetuating symbols of the leading characters.

Wells' journalistic backgrounds caused him to convey the downfall of civilization by showing the gradual deterioration of newspapers. These were supposed to have been supplemented by views of ruined landmarks, but no such shots exist now.

Cabal, incarcerated by Boss Rudolph, originally delivered a monologue that made apparent his high standing in "Wings Over the World." This speech would have clarified a few points about Cabal, but the character who actually suffers most in this segment of the film is Dr. Harding. His sardonic observations on the complete degeneration of mankind have, in the final version, been reduced to: "There is nothing that will make anyone comfortable anymore!"

Young Gordon's actual escape is edited so that we see him flying away from Everytown. We do not see the scenes involving the frightened guard who accompanies him to Basra; also missing is Gordon's appearance before the Council of "Wings Over the World." At this point there's also a minor hole in Wells' script: Boss Rudolph seeks Dr. Harding's help against gas, without any mention, in his presence, of anything to do with the "Gas of Peace." It is doubtful that he recognized Cabal's huge headpiece as a gasmask, or he would have used it himself.

Everything following the Reconstruction phase of the film was completely reworked. The book speaks of the final years as the 2050's whereas the film shows the entire action occurring in 2036. Interestingly, one of the interim titles for the film was "One Hundred Years to Come," and 2036 would have marked a full century after the release date.

Ernest Thesiger was originally scheduled to play the part of

Theotocopulos, but was replaced by Sir Cedric Hardwicke (probably because of Thesiger's 1935 role of "Dr. Praetorius" in *The Bride of Frankenstein*). His scenes had to be reshot and the role, as a result, was probably reworked for Hardwicke's style. Thesiger, however, did appear as "Rev. Maydig" in *Things to Come*'s companion film, *The Man Who Could Work Miracles*.

A long scene between Oswald Cabal and Passworthy was planned, in which they exchanged their views of life, honor and dynamism. Followed by a tour through a vast, futuristic gymnasium, this led into a discussion with their children about the coming flight around the moon. In all probability the live-action footage of these scenes was shot, but the miniatures and opticals would have been too much additional expense and work. The scenes exist in current prints of the film, reedited so that both discussions seem to be taking place in one location. Photographs exist of Cabal and Passworthy talking in another location, and of their children passing through huge rooms, apparently on their way to meet them.

Even though science has built up the world of 2036, there are artists who fear their works of art are being dwarfed by the incredibly vast devices of the scientists. Theotocopulos is the core of this school of thought. In the finished film he appears as a malcontent who makes one short speech over worldwide television, promptly inciting rebellion. In the script, though, we're presented with a more thorough treatment. Theotocopulos' speech is revealed to be much longer and specific, coming to grips with such issues as religion vs. science. Wells' view on this matter was anything but orthodox.

Instead of worrying about religion being obsolete in the age of science, Theotocopulos theorizes that science itself has evolved into a sort of monomania, religious in its fervor, that draws man's attention away from the creative forces of art. Wells implies that either the future world had indeed overlooked religion in favor of science, or that religion *was* a surviving factor being used by this revolutionary figure to corrupt the populace against science. Since there *is* no mention of anything resembling religion, except in this speech, it is probable that Wells wished to show that future human beings will be so secure in their own increased specific understanding of the universe, they would have no use for anything as abstract as organized religion. One feels that Wells regarded denominational religion as a sort of "security blanket," indicative of man's infancy, to be discarded before man could learn to live by universal scientific concepts.

If Wells' religious theories were radical, his views of women must have been regarded as downright revolutionary. In the original script he had built up a carefully constructed geneology outlining the changing concepts of the "acceptable" woman throughout future ages.

In his opening remarks in *The King Who Was a King,* Wells stated his theories on the "love interest," and upon women in general:

The film entrepreneur having given his imaginative author carte blanche is apt to return upon his tracks with afterthoughts. Among the trade and professional solicitudes that haunt him, one is predominant. He has to secure the services of a starry lady. More than half the normal audience is feminine. He insists they must find themselves in the film, and from this point of view this can only be done by introducing a "love interest." Our hero must have his sufficiently difficult task further complicated by the dire attractiveness of blue eyes or brown — or both. A normal love interest should have been kept out of this film. It will either be a triviality or a fatal interruption.[2]

And later:

Women can listen to sexless music and compose and play sexless music; they can do scientific research, produce art and literature, give themselves to sport or business, without even as much direct sex obsession as many men betray. It is, however, not quite so certain that they can lose sight of their own personalities as completely as men can do. If women are no more sexual than men, it is nevertheless open to question whether they can release themselves as readily from a personal reference. My own impression is that, typically, they see the role more and the play less.[3]

From these remarks, it seems that Wells expected to be compelled to include a "normal love interest," which he defined as:

. . . the story of a man strongly attracted by a woman, or vice versa, and the success or failure of a sustained effort to possess her, the price paid and the good or bad delivery. This is currently assumed to be the chief motive in human life, and certainly it is that in the conventional film story.[4]

To cloud his screenplay with a "normal" love interest would have been most distasteful to Wells. Instead, he injected a "symbolic" love affair, tracing Cabals' various relationships with women and illustrating the evolution of male-female sociological interplay.

Young John Cabal's wife is a gentle, timid woman, afraid of what will become of her family in the event of war. The aged John Cabal comes into contact with Roxana Black, a very different type of female. The script contained herein contains a monologue in which John Cabal, over Roxana's unconscious body, speaks of her as an eternal adventuress who influences the destinies of those around her. This is not all complimentary, as he insinuates that Roxana is a "leech;" he wonders if there will be any place for her kind in the world of the future. This monologue was filmed, but is missing from surviving prints.

The script specifies that some of the "Wings Over the World" paratroopers are women, wearing uniforms identical to the men. Again, photos exist of this, but the women do not show up in the film.

Though Roxana Black's character is sufficiently developed in the film, the dialogue comparing her aggressive type to Mary Harding's loving wife portrayal has been eliminated. This is consistent with the cuts of Roxana's futuristic counterpart, Rowena. However, John Cabal's dialogue with Roxana is left intact, and it leads one to wonder just when the decision was made to edit the Rowena footage, especially since the film's opening credits, even in surviving prints, credit actress Margaretta Scott with playing "Roxana" and "Rowena."

Rowena is the erstwhile wife of World President Oswald Cabal. In their dialogue, Cabal accuses her of being the same "eternal adventuress" type as Roxana, enjoying independence for the purpose of bettering her own physical position in the face of the world. Rowena shares Theotocopulos' conviction that science is influencing Cabal to the point of monomania. She still loves Cabal, and Cabal still admits an attachment for her. In admitting this affection, he also admits there may well be a degree of wisdom in her observations.

The relationship between these two is the final "growing pain" in Wells' scale of female social evolution. Their daughter, Catherine, is working with society. She has become a part of it to the extent that she's one of the first two space explorers. She is a female extension of Cabal's driving force. The onlooker gets the impression that the next generation will probably consist of men and women working completely together, on the same levels, each enjoying the reciprocal respect of the other.

Wells succeeded in creating the basis for a great film: a treatment composed mostly of sheer eloquence in idea and delivery. *Things to Come* cannot be said to be overly optimistic, for it depicted World War II dragging on into the last part of the 1900's, almost causing the downfall of civilization. Nor was it overly pessimistic, for the world was successfully rebuilt to eliminate disease and the "ugly spectacle of waste" of the old way of life. In the end, the followers of Theotocopulos were unable to destroy the Spacegun. They had to live with science. Many people were probably killed by the concussion of the Gun: Cabal's warnings were probably remembered in lieu of Theotocopulos' tirades.

Throughout his introduction to this filmscript, Wells makes it clear that he intends *Things to Come* to be the antithesis of Fritz Lang's film *Metropolis*. Far from having man lost amid science, Wells first shows humanity falling victim to its "toys" of destruction, then finally finding the wisdom to hold its knowledge in check and use it for human advancement and comfort.

In the final analysis, Wells presents us with anticipations of horror that mushroom into full cataclysm. He attempts to project the logical course and consequences developing from these conflicts. He reinforces this all with the hope that man *would* have the wisdom to recognize the scope of his true identity, and finally direct himself into a constructive and symbolic thrust "at last, out across immensity to the stars."

The project is anything but egotistical; after formulating his prophecies, Wells turns his work of scientific speculation into an editorial question that has not been answered to this day.

There is one single, most important fact regarding Wells' screenplay for *Things to Come.* No matter how much speculation is lavished upon the accuracy and merit of his effort, there is the inevitable conclusion that the film causes one to watch, listen and question. *Things to Come* justifies itself by achieving the purpose of all films. It entertains.

Allan Asherman
New York

REFERENCES

1. United Artists/London Films issued "The Advertiser's Campaign Manual for *Things to Come*" in 1936, and this publicity kit or "press book" is a source of much valuable background information on the film. Press books are commonly issued by film distributors to help theater owners advertise the films they show. They usually contain posters, display cards, advertising layouts and mats, program notes, and, often, news releases.

2. *The King Who Was a King* (Garden City, N.Y.: Doubleday, Doran, 1929), pp. 27 - 28.

3. *Ibid.,* p. 29.

4. *Ibid.,* p. 28.

THINGS TO COME

Cast

John Cabal, Oswald Cabal .... Raymond Massey
"Pippa" Passworthy,
Raymond Passworthy .... Edward Chapman
Rudolph; The Boss .... Sir Ralph Richardson
Roxana Black, Rowena Cabal .... Margaretta Scott
Theotocopulos .... Sir Cedric Hardwicke
Doctor Harding .... Maurice Braddell
Mrs. John Cabal .... Sophie Stewart
Richard Gordon .... Derek DeMarney
Mary (Harding) Gordon .... Ann Todd
Catherine Cabal .... Pearl Argyle
Maurice Passworthy .... Kenneth Villiers
Morden Mitani .... Ivan Brandt
The Child .... Anne McLaren
The Airman .... John Clements
Simon Burton .... Anthony Holles
Grandfather Cabal .... Alan Jeayes
Horrie Passworthy .... Pickles Livingston
Janet Gordon .... Patricia Hilliard
Wadsky .... Abraham Sofaer

Credits

Screenplay by .... H. G. Wells
Produced by .... Sir Alexander Korda
Directed by .... William Cameron Menzies
Photography by .... Georges Perinal

Settings Designed by . . . Vincent Korda, Moholy Nagy
Special effects directed by .... Ned Mann
Special effects photographer .... Edward Cohen
Assistant to special effects .... Lawrence Butler
Special effects technician .... Harry Zech
Music by .... Sir Arthur Bliss
Musical director .... Muir Matheson
Production Manager .... David B. Cunynghame
Edited by .... William Hornbeck
Astronomical advice .... Nigel Tangye
Costumes designed
by .... John Armstrong, Rene Hubert
Assistant art director .... Frank Wells
Recording engineer .... A. W. Watkins

Running time: 113 minutes
English title: THE SHAPE OF THINGS TO COME
A London Film Production, released by United Artists
Re-released in America in 1947 (Film Classics) and 1965
  (Comet Films)

Scenes from the film *Things to Come*

(All stills are from the collection of Allan Asherman)

1. Artist Austin Briggs' finished advertising layout for the 1936 release of the film in the United States.

2. The ruined "Everytown" set, built on the back lot of Korda's studios.

3. Citizens of "Everytown" in 1970 witness the arrival of John Cabal's airship. Shown left to right are Mary Gordon (Ann Todd), Richard Gordon (Derek DeMarney), Boss Rudolph (Sir Ralph Richardson), Roxana Black (Margaretta Scott), and Doctor Harding (Maurice Braddell).

4. John Cabal (Raymond Massey) emerges from his airship in "Everytown".

5. Boss Rudolph (Sir Ralph Richardson, center): "I am the law here." Cabal (Raymond Massey) smiles as Roxana (Margaretta Scott) looks on anxiously.

6. The Gas of Peace loosed on Boss Rudolph and his followers.

7. "Dead and his world dead with him" proclaims John Cabal (Raymond Massey) over the body of Boss Rudolph (Sir Ralph Richardson).

8. John Cabal (Raymond Massey) makes plans at Wings Over the World head-quarters in Basra.

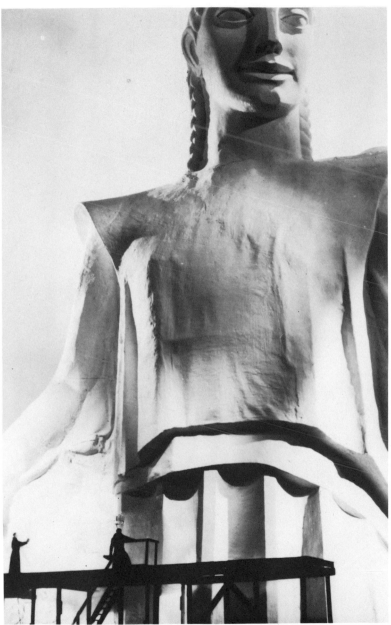

9. Theotocopulos (Sir Cedric Hardwicke) and assistant finish one of the huge statues that decorate the "Everytown" of 2036.

10. Little Girl: "What a funny place New York was — all sticking up and full of windows." Old Man: "They built houses like that in the old days."

11. The reconstructed "Everytown" of 2036.

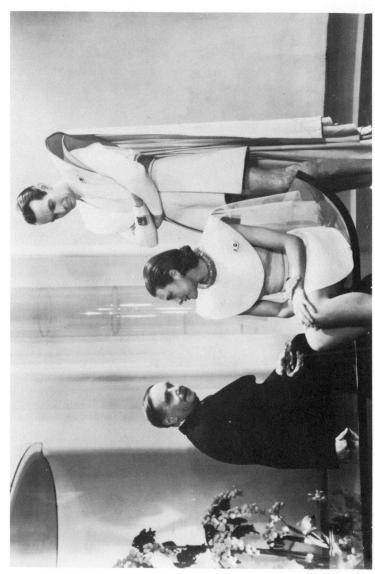

12. H.G. Wells visiting the set of *Things to Come* with Raymond Massey and Pearl Argyle.

13. Rowena Cabal (Margaretta Scott): her scenes were filmed and then edited from the final print of *Things to Come*.

14. Ned Mann's miniature Space-Gun set: the gun itself was over ten feet tall.

15. Hoardes of people storm the Space-Gun in 2036 (A miniature set: the figures are set on tiny conveyor belts).

16. "All the universe . . . or nothingness. Which shall it be, Passworthy, which shall it be?" (Raymond Massey and Edward Chapman).

Introduction

THINGS TO COME was the first great science fiction sound film, as ambitious in its time (1936) as *2001: A Space Odyssey* (1971). Like almost all science fiction films, good and bad, it was overpraised or unfairly condemned, and continues to be so. Unlike Stanley Kubrick's film, it was a financial failure even after many years of release. Yet it was the first science fiction film which succeeded substantially in meeting the standards necessary to have a good science fiction film, rather than a good work of cinema by itself. I would like to point out the considerable virtues of *Things to Come,* while keeping in mind the various fronts on which most science fiction films fail.

To begin with, the film has a strong *screen play,* which is acted by giants, characters who speak out against each other and against their fate with classical passion. The anti-war ideas and sentiments are of historic interest in light of the war that followed and especially in light of the Vietnam conflict whose end was promised again and again (and is not yet ended for the Vietnamese), much like the repeated promises of the Chief in Wells' film. The film also embraces such ideas as humankind remaking the earth; the insistence on law *and* sanity; the love of reaching for the stars, of risking comfort for something creative in us; the sensitivity to human waste and ignorance; the ascetic, apolitical superman who is calm, saving his passion for only the most worthy ends. All these things, which belong so clearly to what many of us who write and know science fiction think of as a worthwhile future, make the film a unique expression of general attitudes which surely belong in any good future.

But the film is rich in more than this. It rises to a special brilliance beyond the virtues of right-thinking. John Baxter is on strong ground when he writes:

The most remarkable quality of *Things to Come* is the coherence and consistency of its design. Menzies may not have been a master of direction, but his sense of balance and mastery of what Eisenstein called "visual counterpoint" has never been better displayed than in this film. Concerned only in the most general way with textures and movements within the frame, Menzies puts his whole effort into the balance of his sets, the conflict between masses, and the choreography of matter. His designs fill the frame both vertically and horizontally, while the use of the low angle sends individual groupings surging out at the audience.[1]

Baxter should say at this point that the film's design supports the expression of its ideas and theme. But, believing that ideas are unsuited to science fiction film, he makes no mention of the integration of its visual expression with its science fictional content. Of special excellence in design/content integration is the final sequence at the reflecting telescope, as Cabal (played by Raymond Massey) and Passworthy (Edward Chapman) catch a fleeting glimpse of the space vehicle which has recently been launched to the moon. The scene is side lighted, giving the character's faces a dark edge which contrasts with the white telescope and dark, starry heavens. One could easily make a case for the explicit symbolism of man's backward and forward looking natures in the half darkened faces. The scene has been called the archetypal science fictional moment on film.

Passworthy asks: "If they don't come back — my son and your daughter — what of that, Cabal?"

"Then, presently, others will go," Cabal says calmly.

"Oh, God, is there never to be any age of happiness? Is there never to be any rest?" (This question comes after we have seen a century of struggle to achieve a just standard of living on the earth.)

"Rest enough for the individual man — too much, and too soon, and we call it Death. But for Man no rest and no ending . . . . First this little planet with its winds and ways, and then all the laws of mind and matter that restrain him. Then the planets about him, and at last out across immensity to the stars. And when he has conquered all the deeps of space and all the mysteries of time, still he will be beginning."

"But . . . we're such little creatures. Poor humanity's so fragile, so weak. Little . . . little animals."

"Little animals. If we're no more than animals we must snatch each little scrap of happiness and live and suffer and pass, mattering no more than all the other animals do or have done." John Cabal points to the reflection of space in the telescope's mirror. "Is it this — or that: all the universe or nothing. Which shall it be, Passworthy? Which shall it be?"

Baxter writes:

Over this dialogue Bliss imposes a soft but powerful melody, building with the intensity of Cabal's speech until the full orchestra and choir surge up at the end with an echo of his final question . . . The final scene is a triumph of music and image. The hard side lighting and almost stylised close-ups of Massey's face, his impeccable delivery of what is basically a technocratic credo and Bliss's profoundly moving music combine to give it a unique quality of optimism and dignity.[2]

Baxter again fails to take his statements about the film, and what they imply about all science fiction film, to their logical conclusion. His thesis about the incompatibility of the film medium with ideas is a strait jacket. He might have continued the passage quoted above by saying that music has always had the quality of transcendence and striving, qualities which lend themselves easily to an association with the *ideas* of good science fiction. Wells-Korda-Menzies employed Sir Arthur Bliss, the English composer, to create a serious score for *Things to Come.* But it was Kubrick who continued the promise of serious music for science fiction film by making use of the intuition, held by many in science fiction, that the music already existed. At the same time he gave new life to the older works he selected. The music in both films expresses what Baxter calls "the essential spirit of science fiction."[3] Most importantly, the music supports the movement of ideas belonging to good science fiction, generally the ideas of change and creativity. I bring this point up to show one of the ways in which ideas may be expressed in a science fiction film, in contrast to Baxter who says they cannot and asks us to take his word for it.

Baxter grants that *Things to Come* is "rich in the essential spirit of science fiction," but he continues with hopelessly vague attacks on the film, using unsupported phrases like "politically and sociologically specious," and sneering at the film for advocating "a mild and undemanding happiness" in its view of the future. (The film does not actually do this; rather, there is a continuing dialogue in which this is *one* of the positions.) He finds Wells' future dull and unworkable, missing the point that no blueprint or visionary work of art can ever be the actual future.

What is puzzling in the tired, sloppy criticism this film too often receives is that the exact opposite is happening on the screen to what the critics say is happening. The innovative characters in the film are in fact unhappy with what material comfort is doing to the creative impulses of their culture, and are seeking change.

What is important in the ideas of *Things to Come,* an understanding of which the thesis of Baxter's book prevents him from approaching with any perceptive enterprise, is that Wells wanted his audiences to accept not his specifics, which belong only to the world of the film's story, but the general constructive attitudes — the idea that the future must be an object of creative concern, that futures are to be *made, invented,* not passively predicted. "The essential spirit of science fiction" has always stood for alternatives, not for any one party line future. The dull Wellsian utopia that Baxter complains about in the tired phrases of anti-scientific humanistic scholasticism is demonstrably not static. We see it being shaken up by the conflict over the space venture which is the film's finale.

In a profound display of complexity, Wells' script delves into the issue of jealousy between creativity in the arts, and in science and technology. It has been said that the secret fear of humanists is that the sciences will claim the energies of the best and brightest, thus making art and literature obsolete while plunging the world into a technological dark age. But despite the appearance that the best intellects go into science, there are many who do not, and many more (among them writers of science fiction) who refuse to take up adversary positions. The world's great scientists number among our greatest humanists, while many non-scientists in other fields are scientifically literate. Only the second-raters sneer at each other.[4] What is amusing in Baxter's arguments against the ideas of *Things to Come* (while claiming at the same time that science fiction film cannot express ideas) is that his hostile position resembles the one held in the film by the barbarian Chief, who expressed a terrified suspicion of "technical chaps," as he calls them. Most negative reactions to the film, and to Wells' life work, show the same fragmentation of energies and concerns.

This conflict is a modern one, and still with us. As in the film, it is a challenge to further growth, striking directly at the continuing viability of the species that inhabits the blue marble our astronauts saw as they looked back from the moon. That the idea of space travel should be pitted against the reality of human welfare on earth, and in 1936, is proof that even in his last decade Wells had an historical imagination of the first order.

Even the much ridiculed electric cannon which launches the spacecraft in the film is a much more sophisticated invention than many know about. (Another complaint about the film is that it lacks genuine technological innovations.) It is not a simple Vernian cannon, which would compress the astronauts into pulp with the sudden acceleration of firing. It is a "graduated electric catapult" in the shape of a cannon within a cannon, which would accelerate the vehicle by stages. The design is reportedly the work of Willy Ley, the rocket expert. Both the U.S. and the the Soviet Union have at one time considered the economics of such ground based and powered booster systems.

Wells could not sneer at "whole wheat" utopias in a world where so much was lacking. He had a sense of priorities. Wells scholars have been gradually freeing his name of the taint of technocracy and scientism which has been imposed on him by proponents of the "two cultures" myth. *Things to Come* is rich in ideas as well as being an excellent film, demonstrating to the careful viewer that concepts are an important part of good science fiction film, and that written science fiction is not hopelessly at odds with the film medium. Baxter's thesis about science fiction film can be disproven by any resourceful script writer-director team deciding to do so. His attack on *Things to Come* and Wells collapses very easily, built as it is of second-hand assertions representing a superficial and antiquated view of the historical Wells.

The successful play of ideas in the film can be demonstrated even briefly. They show a unified movement without which the film's images would be diminished. The visual counterpoint is paralleled by a counterpoint of ideas. A tug-of-war goes on in the film between Wellsian social ideas and Vernian technological elements, between the didactic and romantic elements of science fiction. On the one hand there is a concern with the improvement of human life in practical, material engineering terms; and on the other hand there is a concern with the ineffable, the aesthetic, the noble and the transcendent. All these things are present in what we see and hear. In every scene the film shows the intrusion of the unknown and dangerous into the known and limited — the sort of thing which every now and then pushes our imaginations into new realms, and without which life would not be worth living. It is this attitude which Wells tried to harness to the remaking of the world. He did not have to succeed with the world, nor be a perfect prophet with a workable scheme on the screen, to make this a great science fiction film — which it is because it does everything necessary to such a work.

Where *Things to Come* falls short is in its model work, which is inferior to that in Fritz Lang's earlier silent film, *Metropolis* (1927). For all its visual beauty, however, Lang's film fails as *science fiction* film because it says so little — not much more than an inconclusive political statement that factory workers and owners are heart, mind and muscle, and should cooperate. The story and characters carry no conviction or reality. The ending is ludicrous. Even at its most simplistic, *Things to Come* projects a sense of open possibility absent from *Metropolis,* which is a technological gothic. Its excellences lie elsewhere.[5] *Things to Come* has a strong grasp of the polar opposites of safety and adventure, of boredom and novelty, of consolidation and innovation. Its finale sums up much of science fiction — in this case capturing the moment when a hard-won future state of affairs is about to be surpassed by further progress.

Wells was a *critic* of progress, not simply an advocate. In *Things to Come* we are made to feel dramatically, intellectually and *visually* that the overall pattern of change cannot be grasped in advance, except momentarily; and that beyond the attainment of social welfare lies the problem without end, the question of what to live for. This problem exists deeply in human nature, and is a source of pessimism about humanity. Wells' answer is in creative ventures of our own choice, made possible by the dull comfort of material welfare which many scorn. Wells saw the dangers of technological plenty, and the desirability of making danger and dying worthwhile. That his filmscript should present this problem along with the outward-looking dream of space travel constitutes a mature vision unencumbered by despair and the frustrations of solipsism which World War II was to place over his mental life like a shroud.

Today, *Things to Come* requires a certain amount of innocence to be seen properly, the ability to hold still long enough to enable our imaginations to see past the film's dated aspects to the universal problems which are still with us. Only then will we see that Wells did not promise us a future without problems, but one of continuing human achievement, requiring the utmost of human intelligence, feeling and ethical concern. He offered not *the* future but "The Shape of Things to Come" (the film's other title). He stated this approach quite clearly in 1902:

It is possible to believe that all the human mind has ever accomplished is but the dream before the awakening. We cannot see, and there is no need for us to see, what the world will be like when the day has fully come. But it is out of our race and lineage that minds will spring, that will reach back to us in our littleness to know us better than we know ourselves, and that will reach forward fearlessly to comprehend this future that defeats our eyes. All this world is heavy with the promise of greater things, and a day will come, one day in the unending succession of days, when beings, beings who are now latent in our thoughts and hidden in our loins, shall stand upon this earth as one stands upon a footstool, and shall laugh and reach out their hands amidst the stars.[6]

It is the excruciatingly beautiful sense of change, of transition and metamorphosis, as seen through the eyes of critical intellect and knowledge, that is the heart of good science fiction. *Things to Come* exemplifies this clearly, showing us that (to paraphrase Stanisław Lem) miracles can be cruel as well as beautiful, and that humankind, no matter how frail and fallible, believes itself to be invincible. Wells believed, against his pessimism, that an alliance of reason and good will would at least insure a large measure of success, if not quite perfection; while at the same time he feared that technical progress and plenty would ruin us. *Things to Come* was his last large effort to tell us that even if we reach beyond our grasp, we will grasp enough in the effort. He tried to see past the coming war whose shadow is cast backward in time into the beautifully lighted images of this classic film.

George Zebrowski
Johnson City, N.Y.

REFERENCES

1. John Baxter, *Science Fiction in the Cinema* (International Film Guide Series, New York: A. S. Barnes & Co., 1970), pp. 62 - 63.

2. *Ibid.*, p. 62.

3. Despite Stanley Kubrick's reported contempt for *Things to Come* (see Arthur C. Clarke, The Lost Worlds of 2001 [New York: Signet Books, 1972]), the "choreography of matter" complete with music is also a virtue of *2001.*

4. Arthur C. Clarke once remarked that he had never known a first-rate scientist to make fun of science fiction, while lesser ones do. On the humanities side, science fiction writers are often gleefully "identified" as fifth column technocrats in league with those other philistines, the think tankers and futurists.

5. For a more thorough discussion of this film and others, see my chapter, "Science Fiction and the Visual Media," in Reginald Bretnor, ed., *Science Fiction, Today and Tomorrow* (New York: Harper & Row, 1974) — which is also available from Penguin Books in paperback. Much of my discussion of *Things to Come* here is based on this earlier discussion.

6. H. G. Wells, "The Discover of the Future," *Nature* 65 (1902), 331.

THINGS TO COME

Mr. Wells has also written the following novels:

The Wheels of Chance
Love and Mr. Lewisham
Kipps
Tono-Bungay
Ann Veronica
The History of Mr. Polly
The New Machiavelli
Marriage
The Passionate Friends
The Wife of Sir Isaac Harman

Bealby
The Research Magnificent
Mr. Britling sees it Through
The Soul of a Bishop
Joan and Peter
The Secret Places of the Heart
Christina Alberta's Father
The World of William Clissold
Meanwhile
The Bulpington of Blup

The following Fantastic and Imaginative Romances:

The Time Machine
The Wonderful Visit
The Island of Dr. Moreau
The Invisible Man
The War of the Worlds
The Sleeper Awakes
The First Men in the Moon
The Sea Lady
The Food of the Gods
In the Days of the Comet

The War in the Air
The World Set Free
The Undying Fire
Men Like Gods
The Dream
Mr. Blettsworthy on Rampole Island
The King who was a King
The Autocracy of Mr. Parham
The Shape of Things to Come

Numerous Short Stories collected under the following titles:

The Stolen Bacillus
The Plattner Story

Tales of Space and Time
Twelve Stories and a Dream

The same short stories will also be found collected in one volume under the title: The Short Stories of H. G. Wells, *which also contains* The Time Machine.

A series of books on Social, Religious and Political Questions:

Anticipations (1900)
The Discovery of the Future
A Modern Utopia
The Future in America
New Worlds for Old
First and Last Things
God the Invisible King
The Outline of History
Russia in the Shadows
The Salvaging of Civilisation
Washington and the Hope of Peace
A Short History of the World

The Story of a Great Schoolmaster
A Year of Prophesying
The Way the World is Going
The Science of Life
The Work, Wealth and Happiness of
    Mankind
What are we going to do with our
    Lives?
After Democracy
The New America: The New World
    (*published by* The Cresset Press)

Two Little Books about Children's Play called:

Floor Games *and* Little Wars

and :

Experiment in Autobiography (*published by* The Cresset Press and Victor Gollancz)

THINGS TO COME

H. G. WELLS

A FILM STORY BASED ON
THE MATERIAL CONTAINED
IN HIS HISTORY OF THE
FUTURE "THE SHAPE OF
THINGS TO COME"

LONDON
THE CRESSET PRESS
11 FITZROY SQUARE, W.1
1935

THE JACKET FOR THIS BOOK
HAS BEEN DESIGNED BY
E. MCKNIGHT KAUFFER

Printed in Great Britain by
THE SHENVAL PRESS

CONTENTS

INTRODUCTORY REMARKS   9

PART 1   BEFORE THE SECOND WORLD WAR   19

2   THE SHADOW OF WAR UPON EVERYTOWN   20

3   JOHN CABAL'S—CHRISTMAS EVE   22

4   WAR BREAKS OVER EVERYTOWN   28

5   THE SECOND WORLD WAR   32

6   THE TWO AIRMEN   34

7   THE UNENDING WAR   37

8   THE WANDERING SICKNESS   39

9   EVERYTOWN UNDER A PATRIOT CHIEF   47

10   RECONSTRUCTION   91

11   THE LITTLE GIRL LEARNS ABOUT THE NEW
WORLD   94

12   THE NEW GENERATION   98

13   WORLD AUDIENCE   119

14   THE STRUGGLE FOR THE SPACE GUN   127

15   THE FIRING OF THE SPACE GUN   135

16   FINALE   141

Introductory Remarks

THIS is essentially a spectacular film. It shows the world devastated by modern warfare, the fabric of society shattered, and the world depopulated by a new pestilence, the Wandering Sickness, of which the peculiar horror is that the sufferer, like a sheep stricken with the gid, wanders infectiously until death ends the wandering. The pestilence completes the social disorganisation wars have begun. Mankind, however, is not exterminated by this sickness; some types are immune and among these there are many who remember the order and science of their earlier years. The fall of modern civilisation has been very swift, a matter of a few decades; the flourishing time, the rich promise, of the opening twentieth century is still remembered, and so, after an interlude during which most regions of the earth have fallen under the barbaric sway of warring brigand chiefs, the men of knowledge and technicians, and more particularly the aviators and transport engineers, get together, revive the old mechanisms, take control and build up a new civilisation upon rational lines. This time it is a World Pax they create, for most of the political landmarks and limitations of our present time have been washed out by forty years of confusion. And it is a scientific order of society; for what other alternative to perpetual conflict can the future hold for us?

The book upon which this story rests, *The Shape of Things to Come*, is essentially an imaginative *discussion* of social and political forces and possibilities, and a film is no place for argument. The conclusions of that book therefore are taken for granted in this film, and a new story has been invented to display them, a story woven first about the life of one man,

John Cabal, who is an aviator, who passes unscathed
through both war and epidemic and becomes the stalwart
grey-haired leader and inspiration of the air men, and then
in the second part, about his grandson, Oswald Cabal, head
of the world council, and a living embodiment of the spirit
of human adventure, who finds himself in a new conflict with
the conservative and reactionary elements that are still
strong in the human community.

The film moves swiftly through opening scenes of warfare,
destruction and deepening misery, and broadens out to
display the grandiose spectacle of a reconstructed world.
Mankind, by a great moral and intellectual effort, has
solved the main economic and social perplexities that distress
us to-day, and lives either upon a cleansed and beautiful
countryside or in great, half-subterranean cities, bedded in
the hills, flooded with artificial light and sweet and clean
with perfectly conditioned air. The surplus energies of the
race spend themselves upon constructive and creative art and
science. Incessant exploration is the essential thing in science,
and some of the young and more adventurous spirits have
become urgent to reach out to the moon. On this the drama
of the concluding portion turns. Cabal's daughter and her
lover, Maurice Passworthy, have volunteered to be the first
human beings to leave the earth on the moon voyage, they
have been accepted on account of their exceptional fitness,
and Cabal is torn between instinctive tenderness and heroic
exaltation. The expedition has roused a widespread opposi-
tion among the more æsthetic types in the community, who
resent the sternness of the rule of the men of science and are
in revolt against what they regard as the wanton exposure of
young and beautiful people to danger, hardship and death.
An eloquent poet and artist, Theotocopulos, leads the people
in this new revolt. He clamours for a return to what he calls

"the simple natural life of man." So the film culminates in a conflict, about a gigantic "Space Gun," between the human conservative instincts and human courage and adventurousness, and it ends in a note of interrogation among the stars.

Note to the Reader

THIS was the first film "Treatment" written by the Author for actual production, and he found much more difficulty in making it than he did in any of its successors. He learnt his trade upon it. His previous effort in film writing, a silent film, *The King who was a King*, was an entirely amateurish effort which never reached the screen. What is before the reader here is the last of several drafts. An earlier treatment was made, discussed, worked upon for a little and discarded. It was a prentice effort and the author owes much to the friendly generosity of Alexander Korda, Lajos Biro, and Cameron Menzies, who put all their experience at his disposal during this revision. They were greatly excited by the general conception, but they found the draft quite impracticable for production. A second treatment was then written. This, with various modifications, was made into a scenario of the old type. This scenario again was set aside for a second version, and this again was revised and put back into the form of the present treatment. Korda and the author had agreed upon an innovation in film technique, to discard the elaborate detailed technical scenario altogether and to produce directly from the descriptive treatment here given. We have found this work very well in practice—given a competent director. By this time, however, the author, now almost through the toils of apprenticeship, was in a state of fatigue towards the altered, revised and reconstructed text, and, though he has done his best to get it into tolerable film prose he has an uneasy sense that many oddities and awkwardnesses of expression that crept in during the scenario have become now so familiar to him that he has become blind to them and has been unable to get rid of them.

The Music

THE music is a part of the constructive scheme of the film, and the composer, Mr. Arthur Bliss, was practically a collaborator in its production. In this as in many other respects, this film, so far at least as its intention goes, is boldly experimental. Sound sequences and picture sequences were made to be closely interwoven. This Bliss music is not intended to be tacked on; it is a part of the design. The spirit of the opening is busy and fretful and into it creeps a deepening menace. Then come the crashes and confusions of modern war. The second part is the distressful melody and grim silences of the pestilence period. In the third, military music and patriotic tunes are invaded by the throbbing return of the air men. This throbbing passes into the mechanical crescendo of the period of reconstruction. This becomes more swiftly harmonious and softer and softer as greater efficiency abolishes that clatter of strenuous imperfection which was so distinctive of the earlier mechanical civilisation of the nineteenth century. The music of the new world is gay and spacious. Against this plays the motif of the reactionary revolt; ending in the stormy victory of the new ideas as the Space Gun fires and the moon cylinder starts on its momentous journey. The music ends with anticipations of a human triumph in the heroic finale amidst the stars.

It cannot be pretended that in actual production it was possible to blend the picture and music so closely as Bliss and I had hoped at the beginning. The incorporation of original music in film production is still in many respects an unsolved problem. But Bliss's admirable music has also been separately performed and gramophone records of it are obtainable.

Memorandum

Circulated during production to everyone concerned in designing and making the costumes, decoration, etc., for the concluding phase (A.D. 2055) of "Things to Come."

THERE are certain principles in this undertaking to be observed, which as yet do not seem to be as clearly grasped as they must be. I make no apology therefore for reiterating these principles now as emphatically as possible.

The first is this, that in the final scenes we are presenting a higher phase of civilisation than the present, where there is greater wealth, finer order, higher efficiency. Human affairs in that more organised world will not be hurried, they will not be crowded, there will be more leisure, more dignity. The rush and jumble and strain of contemporary life due to the uncontrolled effects of mechanism, are not to be raised to the *n*th power. On the contrary they are to be eliminated. Things, structures, in general, will be great, yes, but they will not be monstrous. Men will not be reduced to servitude and uniformity, they will be released to freedom and variety. All the balderdash one finds in such a film as Fritz Lange's *Metropolis* about "robot workers" and ultra skyscrapers, etc., etc., should be cleared out of your minds before you work on this film. As a general rule you may take it that whatever Lange did in *Metropolis* is the exact contrary of what we want done here. Soldiers in the phalanx or in the Zulu impi or in the infantry fighting of the eighteenth century, plantation labourers, galley slaves, early factory workers, peasants, "common people" generally in the past, were infinitely more uniform and "mechanical" than any people of the future will be. Machinery has superseded the subjugation and "mechanisation" of human beings. *Please keep that in mind.* The workers to be shown are individualised workers doing responsible co-operative team work. And *work will be unobtrusive* in the coming civilisation.

So will working costumes. Function will not obtrude. You will not see people rushing about in a monstrous rig, all goggles and padding and gadgets like the early aviators. People will not be plastered over with gadgets as though they had recently looted Mr. Gamage's well-known notion stores. Men and women of the future will carry the equivalents of the purse, pocket book, fountain pen, watch, etc., etc., of to-day, but these things will be unobtrusive and subservient in a graceful decorative scheme. Just as when we were discussing the music for this film we decided that in the reconstruction Part the early phase should be full of effort and mechanical clangour and that this should merge in harmony and almost noiseless running, as the machinery increased in smooth efficiency, so the costumes also must not be *noisy.* People in the future will not be rigged up like telephone poles or as if they had just escaped from some sort of electrical operating room. They will not wear costumes of cellophane illuminated by neon lights or anything extravagant of that sort. Do bear in mind that the most extravagant costumes known in the world are those made by savages for ceremonial dances and the like.

For reasons that I have given again and again—the fact that in the future various light apparatus such as a portable radio, electric torch, notebook, will have to be carried on the person and that this will probably necessitate a widening of those broadly padded shoulders which are already necessary in the costume of contemporary men because of their wallets and fountain pens—I anticipate a costume, broad on the shoulders and fine about the legs and feet, with a fairly simple coiffure, more reminiscent of "Tudor" (Renaissance) style than anything else the world has seen. Fine materials we want but not extraordinary materials. For such a man as Cabal I want a white or silver costume of very pure material. I want him to look a fine gentleman, not a padded lunatic or an armoured gladiator. There will be a radio telephone arrangement on his chest no more obtrusive than a modern breast pocket, and he will wear a long fine gauntlet on one wrist, in which various small conveniences, the equivalent of the contemporary fountain pen, etc., and an identification disk—his introduction card so to speak—will be carried. The identification disk I make a general feature. There may be beautiful embroidery or patterning on his silky clothing.

The released energy of the future is sure to find a considerable outlet in detailed decoration. Passworthy's costume should be highly decorative. Morden Mitani likes the effectiveness of black, Theotocopulos borders on extravagance—a vast cloak, a rich body costume. Clothing will have a *style*, but within the limits of that style it will be very varied. Some women, especially the younger and shapelier, will dress like youths, but there are invincible æsthetic reasons why a certain number of them should have considerable skirts. In a clean indoor city, there will be no hygienic objections to quite long skirts. And the broad shoulders that will rule masculine and (either by contrast or imitation) feminine costume, call aloud for cloaks, the most dramatic of garments.

There we have the guiding rules to observe. These marked out limitations and state a style, but within these limitations and style I would say to *our designers*: "For God's sake let yourselves go." But remember, fine clothes, please ; not nightmare stuff, not jazz. People are not going about in glass jars or aluminium boilers or armour or cellophane. They are not going to dress like super-sandwich men. Nor are they going to encumber themselves with big wigs and stays. Nor be "nudists"—neither Adamites nor angels. Being inventive and original is not being extravagant and silly. Fine clothes and dignified clothes, please, for the new world.

THE FILM

THINGS TO COME

Before the Second World War

THIS is a brief display of contemporary humanity. The opening effect is one of walking and hurrying crowds. Across this appears and fades the legend "Whither Mankind?" A rapid succession of flashes evoke the multitudinousness, the hurry and confused inadequate efficiency of our world. Crowds and cities appear and dissolve into kindred scenes in other places; there are momentary flashes of crowded cities, Paris, Tokio, Milan, Valparaiso, Timbuctoo, Moscow.

One of the following special scenes. Either:—

Crowds crossing Brooklyn Bridge and a great traffic and activity in the river below.

The Tower Bridge open to let a steamer through, the pool full of shipping, the cranes on the wharves active.

Port of Bremen similarly active.

Or traffic and crowds by the Eiffel Tower.

Any one of these scenes will suffice. It should correspond with the one chosen for the end of Part VII, *q.v.*

After such scenes of City activity the screen reminds us of such contrasted activities as: small cultivations, and then sweeping across it large scale harvesting; a peasant cart joggling along a road and then crowded trains and platforms. A peasant's cradle rocks and dissolves into the methodical work of a modern child welfare clinic. A wheelwright melts into a great motor car factory.

The mint is seen printing paper money.

Close up of machines turning out paper money and bank clerks handling bunches of it faster and faster.

A Wall Street or Bourse panic scene follows.

All these are flashes of the briefest possible sort. They are intended to recall to the audience outstanding aspects of the contemporary world by shots of familiar and typical scenes and activities. I believe it would be far better for a competent editor and cutter to piece together this part of the film from pre-existing material. The more bustling and familiar it is the better.

As the flashes follow each other faster and faster, the words WHITHER MANKIND? across the scene fade in again for a moment and then fade out as we pass into the second part, in which the localised and personal story opens.

PART II

The Shadow of War upon Everytown

EVERYTOWN *is* every town. That is to say, it is the average great town of our times. It is backed by a very characteristic skyline of hills which recurs throughout the film to remind us that we are following the fate of one typical population group, and it has a central "place," a big Market Square with big hotels, public buildings, cinemas, kiosks, statuary, tramways, etc.

First, there is a general view of Everytown from a crest above it. In the foreground we see workers going down the hill into the town, and down the hill we see the whole of Everytown, suburbs and Central Square together; it is a clear Christmas Eve.

Then we come to the Central Square in Everytown. It has features recalling Trafalgar Square or a big-town Market Square or a French Grand Place. There is a confluence of trams and buses. The Christmas traffic is active. On one of the chief buildings the moving light sign of a newspaper flashes the latest news. "Europe is arming. . . ."

The camera moves up from the traffic of the Square to this light sign: "Alarming speech by Air Minister ——"

Big shop window full of Christmas toys. Children and mothers admiring.

An autobus stops and people get out of it. On the autobus one sees the usual newspaper posters with a glaring headline about the dangerous international situation. "Straits dispute. Acute situation."

The entrance of a tube station. The usual traffic. A newsvendor stands at the entrance. His placard reads : "Another 10,000 aeroplanes." But he shouts, "All the winners."

In an autobus a young girl opens her paper and glances through the first page, which is full of headlines talking about the war danger. She has only a cursory glance for that stuff; she turns the page and plunges with passionate interest into the fashion article.

During all these scenes, Christmas shoppers and people with packages pass to and fro. It is a peaceful and fairly happy Christmas shopping crowd. Nobody appears to be affected imaginatively by the war danger. The voice has called "Wolf" too often. Only the camera calls the attention of the audience to the brooding threat.

At this point the essential story of the film begins.

A glimpse is given of a scientific laboratory in which young Harding, a student of two and twenty, is working intently. It is a small, reasonably well-equipped, municipal school laboratory looking out on the Central Square. It is a biological, not a chemical laboratory. Two microscopes are visible and plenty of laboratory glass, taps, etc., but not too many bottles and no retorts. (This laboratory has to appear in a ruinous state later, *sans* glass or breakables.) Through the open window comes the bellowing of the newsvendor. "War crisis!" Harding listens for a moment: "Damn this war nonsense." He closes the window to shut out the sound. He looks at his watch and sets himself to put things away.

At first he is wearing a neat laboratory overall. This he takes off.

A suburban residential road with little traffic and many pleasant detached homes is seen, and Harding walking along it. He approaches a house through a garden gate.

PART III

John Cabal's—Christmas Eve

A RATHER dark study is seen in which John Cabal is musing over a newspaper. The furniture of the room indicates his connection with flying. There is the blade of a propeller over the mantel shelf and a model on the mantel shelf. On the table are some engineering drawings partly covered by the newspaper.

Cabal's arm, with wrist-watch, is resting on the evening paper. He has a habit of drumming with his fingers which is shown here and again later. The camera comes up to the hand and paper.

The headlines show:

"EVENING NEWSLETTER.

London. December 24th, 1940. 1*d*."

Streamer headline: "STRAITS DISPUTE: ACUTE SITUATION."

Column headlines: "ALARMING SPEECH BY AIR MINISTER. ANOTHER 10,000 AEROPLANES NOW."

(This newspaper should be practically a facsimile of the London *Evening Standard*. It should show the customary insets beside the title of the weather forecast and the lighting-up time. It is the Final Night edition and it also announces Closing City Prices.)

Cabal pondering. He looks towards the door. Harding comes in. He approaches Cabal. Harding sees the paper and the headlines.

Cabal: "Hullo, young Harding! You're early."

Harding: "I had finished up. It was too late to begin anything fresh. Why are the newsboys shouting so loud? What is all this fuss in the papers to-night, Mr. Cabal?"

Cabal: "Wars and rumours of wars again."

Harding: "Crying wolf?"

Cabal: "Some day the wolf will come. These fools are capable of anything."

Harding: "What becomes of medical research in that case?"

Cabal: "It will have to stop."

Harding: "That will mess *me* up. It's pretty nearly all I care for. That and Marjorie Home, of course."

Cabal: "Mess you up! Of course it will mess you up. Mess up your work. Mess up your marriage. Mess everything up. My God, if war gets loose again. . . ."

Cabal and Harding turn towards the door as Passworthy walks in.

Passworthy: "Hullo Cabal! Christmas again!" (Sings.) "While shepherds watched their flocks by night, All seated on the ground. . . ."

Cabal nods at the paper. Passworthy takes it up and throws it down with disdain.

Passworthy: "What's the matter with you fellows? Oh, this little upset across the water doesn't mean war. Threatened men live long. Threatened wars don't occur. Another speech by *him*. Nothing in it, I tell you. Just to buck people up over the air estimates. Don't meet war half-way. Look at the cheerful side of things. *You're* all right. Business improving, jolly wife, pretty house."

Cabal: "All's right with the world, eh? All's right with the world. Passworthy, you ought to be called Pippa Passworthy. . . ."

Passworthy: "You've been smoking too much, Cabal. You—you aren't eupeptic . . ." (Walks round and sings.) "No-el! No-el! No-el! . . ."

In Cabal's living-room. Christmas tree with freshly lit candles burning and presents being taken off and distributed. A children's party in progress. Each child is busy in its own way. Horrie Passworthy is donning a child's soldier's "panoply." Timothy is laying out a toy railway system. He is completely absorbed in his work, neither hearing nor seeing anything, working with the intensity of the born builder. A smaller girl and a very small boy enter the picture. They have been attracted by the work and the worker. They stare admiringly. In another corner of the room Horrie, now in full uniform, beats his drum.

Horrie: "Fall in! Fall in!" Three boys fall in behind him. "Quick march!" They march off to the drum taps.

Timothy finishing his layout. He surveys it with a last glance before starting the engine. Horrie enters the picture with his followers. The camera shows only the marching feet of Horrie's followers. Railway system spread out. Horrie's foot kicks aside some part of the system.

Timothy (nervously): "Don't!"

The marching feet pass by. Timothy has but one thought, to save his gadgets. He succeeds. He lays out his railway again. To a little boy: "You work the signals." The little boy sits down happily. To the little girl: "You—you look on." The little girls sits down and plays her part; she admires. Timothy starts his train. The train moves. Timothy is earnestly observing it. The two children are delighted. Drum going. Horrie and his followers return and halt. Horrie stops and thinks.

Horrie: "Make an accident!"

Timothy looks up for a second: "No." Busy with railway.

Horrie: "Make an earthquake!"

Timothy: "No."

Horrie: "Let's have a war."

Timothy: "No."

Horrie goes off reluctantly.

The toy railway. Train going. One of the carriages collapses. It turns over. It has been hit by a wooden pellet. We see four guns being worked by Horrie and his friends. They are delighted. Timothy realises that the whole layout is being bombarded to pieces. He tries to protect the railway with his hands. Protesting desperately: "Don't—stop!" His hand is hit by a projectile. The little girl protests with Timothy.

Horrie directs the firing of the guns. More projectiles hit Timothy. Timothy jumps to his feet and goes to attack Horrie. Horrie rises quickly, Timothy hits him. Horrie disengages himself from Timothy, kicks over the engine and disarranges the rails. Timothy claws hold of him, and they begin a tussle which ends on the ground.

Uproar in the room. By the middle door Mrs. Cabal enters and hurries towards the fighters. By the door from Cabal's study enter Passworthy, followed by Cabal and Harding. Horrie and Timothy fighting. Mrs. Cabal comes up and tries to pull the boys apart.

Mrs. Cabal: "Timothy, Timothy, what's the matter?"

Passworthy grabs Horrie: "Here, young man, what have you been doing?"

Horrie: "I only made a little war on him, daddy—and he didn't play fair."

Passworthy: "Soldiers are to protect us—not to smash up things."

Horrie: "But daddy, a war *must* smash up things."

Passworthy: "You go on sentry duty, see—soldiers are to prevent war, not provoke it."

Horrie obeys reluctantly. Children resuming their activities. Timothy with railway. Horrie doing sentry go, rather sulkily.

Cabal, Passworthy, Harding, Mrs. Cabal and grandfather are on a raised dais at the end of the room.

Passworthy: "They're forgetting their troubles already. Queer things kids are! Flare up in a moment—and then it's all over."

Grandfather: "Nice toys they have nowadays, nice toys. The toys *we* had were simpler. Ever so much simpler. Noah's Arks and wooden soldiers. Nothing so complex as these. I wonder perhaps if sometimes they don't find these new toys a bit too much for them."

Passworthy: "Now that's an idea!"

Grandfather: "Aye. Just an idea."

Mrs. Cabal: "It teaches them to use their hands."

Grandfather: "Well, I suppose their grandchildren will have still more wonderful things. Progress—and progress—I'd like to see—the wonders *they'll* see."

Cabal: "Don't be too sure of progress."

Passworthy: "You—incurable pessimist."

Grandfather: "Well, what's going to stop progress nowadays?"

Cabal: "*War!*"

Passworthy: "Well, firstly, there isn't going to be a war, and secondly, war doesn't stop progress. It stimulates progress."

Cabal ironically: "Yes war's a *highly* stimulating thing. But you can overdo a stimulant. The next dose may be a fatal one. An overdose."

Passworthy, hesitating: "Well, after all, don't we exaggerate about the horrors of war? Aren't we overdoing that song? The last war wasn't as bad as they make out. One didn't worry. Something great seemed to have got hold of you."

Cabal: "Something still greater may get hold of you next time. You're talking through your hat, Passworthy. If we do not end war—war will end us. Everybody says that, millions of people believe it, and nobody does anything. I do nothing ____"

Passworthy: "Well, what can you do?"

Cabal: "Yes, what can we do?"

Passworthy : "Carry on. Carry on, and trust to the commonsense of mankind."

Christmas tree with the candles burnt half-way down.

Christmas tree with candles being extinguished by a maid. Time has passed.

PART IV

War Breaks over Everytown

THE suburban road outside John Cabal's house. Various clocks—one after another—are heard striking midnight. Cabal's house. Door opens. Cabal, Mrs. Cabal, Harding and Passworthy come out. Christmas bells are heard.

Passworthy: "Peace on earth, Goodwill to all men. It is going to be a real old-fashioned Christmas this year. Fresh and a little snow, a nip in the air."

A faint thud is heard. Everybody silent for a moment.

Mrs. Cabal: "What was that? It sounded like a gun."

Passworthy: "No guns about here. Merry Christmas, Cabal—good luck to us for another twelvemonth. The last wasn't so bad. Here's to another year of recovery."

Long shot of road. Suddenly searchlights appear in the sky silhouetting the hill crest. The group at the door observe the searchlights and turn questioningly towards one another.

Mrs. Cabal: "But what are searchlights doing now?"

Passworthy: "Anti-aircraft manœuvres, I expect."

Cabal: "Manœuvres! At Christmas? No!"

Three thuds rather louder mingle with the pealing bells.

Harding: "Listen. Guns again."

The bells cease abruptly. The sound of distant guns becomes quite distinct.

The group—mute suspense. Heavy concussion heard.

After this the noise subsides as though the trouble was drifting away from Everytown. Nobody speaks. From the study the telephone rings. Cabal turns and hurries back into the house, the others go a few steps after him and listen anxiously.

Cabal, heard off: "What, to-night—three o'clock at the Hilltown hangar. I'll be there."

Cabal comes out again to the listening group. "Mobilisation!"

Mrs. Cabal: "Oh—oh God!"

Passworthy: "Perhaps it's only a precautionary mobilisation."

Cabal turns and goes into the house. The others follow.

Cabal's study. They will hear if the radio has anything to say. Cabal turns on radio.

Radio: "The unknown aircraft passed over Seabeach and dropped bombs within a few hundred yards of the waterworks. They then turned seaward again. By this time they had been picked up by the searchlights of the battleship *Dinosaur* and before they could mount out of range she had opened upon them with her anti-aircraft guns. Unfortunately without result."

Passworthy: "That's—that's alarming certainly."

Harding: "Of course everyone has said 'This time there will be no declaration of war.'"

Mrs. Cabal: "Listen!"

The radio resumes, crackling: "We do not yet know the nationality of these aircraft, though of course there can be little doubt of their place of origin. But before all things it is necessary for the country to keep calm. No doubt the losses suffered by the fleet are serious."

Passworthy, interrupting radio: "*What's* that? Losses of the fleet?"

Mrs. Cabal, impatiently: "Listen! Listen!"

Radio: "And it is imperative that the whole nation should at once stand to arms. Orders for a general mobilisation have been issued and the precautionary civilian organisation against gas will at once be put into operation. Ah—

instructions have come to hand. We shall cut off for five minutes and then read you the general instructions. Please call in any friends. Call in everyone you can." Radio ceases.

Cabal, bitterly: "You've got your stimulant, Passworthy. Something great has got you. War has come."

They all look at each other.

Passworthy, to Harding: "I suppose we shall find our marching orders at home. Nothing to do now but get on with it."

Mrs. Cabal: "War! God help us all."

Passworthy and Harding on their way home. Passworthy garrulous. Harding darkly silent.

Passworthy: "My God! If they have attacked without a declaration of war—then it's vengeance. No quarter, it's vengeance. Punishment—punishment—condign—or an end to civilisation for ever. It's just possible it's some mistake. I cling to that. But if *not*—then War to the Knife. It's not a war. It's a fight against dangerous vermin. A vermin hunt without pause or pity. (Flatly.) Good night."

Harding has had nothing to say. He nods good night, stands watching Passworthy for a moment and then rouses himself with a start to go his way.

The Central Square of Everytown. Large anti-aircraft on truck comes into Square. Searchlights being mounted on a roof.

Electric signs going out.

Special service men in badges herding people to shelter.

Belated straggler running across the Square.

Searchlights break out.

Anti-aircraft gun being loaded by the light of a carefully shaded lamp. Faces of the gunners seen closely.

All this is to be very quick and furtive. As lights go down

the lighting changes to silhouette effects and the sounds diminish until at the end there is absolute silence.

Cabal and his wife in the children's nursery. Cabal is buttoning on his airman uniform. He looks at the sleeping children. He turns his head, tormented by the thought of their future.

Mrs. Cabal: "My dear, my dear, are you sorry we—had these children?"

Cabal thinks long. "No. Life must carry on. Why should we surrender life to the brutes and fools?"

Mrs. Cabal: "I loved you. I wanted to serve you and make life happy for you. But think of the things that may happen to them. Were we selfish?"

Cabal draws her to him: "You weren't afraid to bear them —— *We* were children yesterday. We are anxious, but we are not afraid. Really."

Mrs. Cabal nods acknowledgment, but cannot talk because she would cry.

Timothy's bed, with Cabal and his wife standing beside it.

Cabal: "Courage, my dear."

Whispering to himself: "And may that little heart have courage."

A series of flashes recall the flashes of the second part. Everytown is seen in a belated wintry dawn.

Suburban road. Men come from the houses carrying parcels or suitcases and go off towards the station.

A young wife saying good-bye to her husband, who is waiting for a tram.

Bus stop. Men get on the bus with their packages. A sort of forced cheerfulness. Eyebrows raised and a forced smile with the corners of the mouth turned down.

No march music here. None of the elation of 1914. The shuffle, tramp, tramp of the doomed householders.

Passworthy with Horrie in the front garden of his house. Horrie in his uniform of yesterday. Passworthy going out. He puts on an armlet.

Horrie, pointing to the armlet: "Are you an officer, daddy?"

Passworthy: "We've got to do our bit, sonny. We've got to do our bit."

Horrie: "I'm an officer too, daddy."

Passworthy: "That's the spirit, old son. Nothing else for it now. Carry on, sir. Carry on."

The two salute each other in brave burlesque. He lifts his son and kisses him. He goes.

Horrie by himself. He taps his drum. First thoughtfully, and then with more confidence. He beats the drum, begins to hum and marches. Works himself up. Hums louder—sings wordlessly. The beating of his drum passes into marching music which carries on through the next flashes.

Faintly, behind little Horrie appear the shadows of marching troops, keeping step with him and his drumming. They intensify as he fades.

Effect of marching armies.

PART V

The Second World War

THE marching troops become phantom-like and vanish. A peaceful countryside, winter. The same country scene has appeared in Part I, but now everywhere there are signs of war preparation. In the foreground a smooth-flowing river, or lake, that reflects the scene—suddenly the mirror is broken as enormous amphibian tanks crawl up out of the water. A gigantic howitzer suddenly rears itself up from a peaceful field.

Scene from the air. Roadways choked with war material moving up to the front. Closer detail shots of the same scene. Long lines of tanks and caterpillar lorries. Long lines of steel-helmeted men. Lorries full of men. Lorries full of shells. Great dumps of shells. A fantasia of war material in motion.

Chemical factory. Piles of cases being loaded.

The manufacture of gas bombs. The workers all wear gas masks of ghoulish type.

The guns go off. A repetition of some of the foregoing shots —but now the men and guns are no longer moving into action, but *are* in action. Guns being fired, tanks advance firing, battleships firing a broadside, gas hissing out of cylinders.

A gun crew round a gun, passing shells up to the gun.

Beneath an aeroplane a crew fixing bombs.

Squadron after squadron of aeroplanes take to the sky. Everytown is seen with hostile aeroplanes in the sky. An explosion in the foreground fills the scene. As the smoke clears it reveals the suburban road in Everytown in which Passworthy lives, and something small and dark is seen far down the footpath.

We pass up the road and before the shattered garden fence we see little Horrie in his panoply, sprawling dead.

A long silent pause.

Bombs are heard receding in distance.

(This is the first dead body we see on the screen.)

c

Scenes of Everytown being bombed. Sirens, whistles and hooters. Panic working up in Square. Quick flashes of military working anti-aircraft guns. Again to crowded Square, terrified faces looking up. Increased panic. Aeroplanes overhead. Anti-aircraft firing rather helplessly.

A tramcar runs down the street, it lurches and falls sideways across the street. The façade of a gigantic general store falls into the street. The merchandise is scattered and on fire. Window dummies and wounded civilians lie on the pavement.

Bomb bursting in crowded Square. Cinema crashing in ruins.

A bomb bursts a gas main, a jet of flame, the fire spreads.

Officials distributing gas masks, the crowd in a panic. Fight for masks. Official swept off his feet. Long shot of aeroplanes, they distribute gas like a smoke screen. The cloud slowly descends on the town. The gas cloud descends, the guns continue to fire in the darkness. Long shot of the gas cloud descending on and darkening the Square. People in offices and flats trapped by the gas pouring into the windows.

Long shot of the Square, now very misty and dark. No civilians are moving about, but there are a few scattered dead.

PART VI

The Two Airmen

ENEMY airman, a boy of 19, is in the air, distributing gas. Close up of him in his cockpit. He finishes his supply and banks to turn about. He looks up into the sky and discovers he is being attacked. He is plainly apprehensive.

John Cabal in his aeroplane. He is heading for the enemy airman.

Air fight. It is a one-sided fight between a bomber and a swift fighter. Enemy airman crashes. Cabal nose-dives, but straightens out.

Enemy airman crashing. Houses, etc., in the background under the cloud of gas he has spread. (N.B.—This is no part of Everytown, and the familiar skyline, etc., are to play no part in this scene.)

Cabal landing with difficulty. He looks towards enemy aeroplane and then hurries towards it. Fire breaks out in the wrecked machine as Cabal approaches it.

Cabal arrives at enemy aeroplane. Enemy airman staggers out as the flames spread. He is beating out the fire in his smouldering clothing. He staggers and falls. The rest of the scene goes to a flickering light because of the burning aeroplane. Gusts of *black* smoke across picture.

Cabal helps the enemy airman, who is evidently very badly injured. He is as yet too stunned to be in anguish, but he knows he is done for. Cabal settles him fairly comfortably on the ground.

Cabal: "Is that better? My God—but you are smashed up, my boy."

Cabal tries to make him comfortable. He desists and stares at the enemy airman with a sort of blank amazement.

"Why should we two be murdering each other? How did we come to this?"

The gas is drifting nearer to them. The enemy airman points to it. "Go, my friend! This is my gas, and it is a bad gas. Thank you."

Cabal: "But how did we come to this? Why did we let them set us killing each other?"

The enemy airman says nothing, but his expression assents.

Cabal and the airman take their gas masks. Cabal helps the enemy airman with his mask and adjusts it. There is some difficulty due to the airman's broken arm, Cabal desists and has to try again.

Enemy Airman: "Funny if I'm choked by my own poison."

Cabal: "That's all right."

Cabal puts the mask on and then puts his own on. They hear a cry and look up.

Cabal follows their look, and they see a little girl running before the gas. She is already choking and presses a handkerchief to her mouth. The girl, very distressed, runs towards them and hesitates, not knowing which way to go. She is heedless of the two men.

Enemy airman stares, then tears off his mask and holds it out to Cabal. "Here—put it on her."

Cabal hesitates, looks from one to the other.

Enemy Airman: "I've given it to others—why shouldn't I have a whiff myself?"

Cabal puts the mask on the girl, who resists, frightened, and then understands and submits.

Cabal: "Come on, kiddy, this is no place for you. You make tracks that way. *I'll* show you."

Cabal goes off with the girl and then returns into picture to see if the enemy airman has a pistol. He realises that he has not, hesitates, and gives his own pistol to him. "You may want this."

Enemy Airman: "Good fellow—but I'll take my dose."

The enemy airman is left dying in the flickering light of his burning aeroplane. The gas is very near now. The wisps drift towards him. He looks after Cabal and the girl. "I dropped the stuff on her. Maybe I've killed her father and mother. Maybe I've killed all her family. And then I give up my mask to save her. That's funny. Oh! that's really funny. Ha, ha, ha. That—that's a Joke!"

The gas drifts by him and he starts to cough. He remembers Cabal's words. "What fools we airmen have been! We've let them make us fight for them like dogs. Smashed trying to kill her—and then I gave her my mask! Oh God! It's funny. Ha, ha, ha."

His laugh changes to a cough of distress, as the gas envelops and hides him. The cough grows fainter and fainter, and vapour blots out the scene. "I'll take it all—take it all. I deserve it."

He is heard again coughing and panting. Then comes a sharp cry, then a groan of sudden unendurable suffering.

A pistol shot is heard. Silence. The screen is filled with the drifting vapour.

PART VII

The Unending War

A succession of newspaper headings marks the prolongation of the war.

The first newspaper has the same type of heading as the newspaper in Cabal's study before the Children's Party. Open with a close shot on date of paper.

EVENING NEWSLETTER

The weather forecast and the lighting-up time are no longer there. Date is May 20th, 1941. *Price threepence.* In place of "Closing City Prices" is "Prohibition of Speculation," but the paper still claims to be FINAL NIGHT EDITION.

Headline across two columns: THE END IN SIGHT.

Headline across two columns: THE RATIONING SCANDAL.

Sub-head underneath the first heading: BENEFITS OF
BLAKE'S AIR OFFENSIVE.

Text: "The immense efforts and sacrifices of the air force
during the great counter offensive of last month are bearing
fruit."

Camera close up to the date again and the close up to the
date is repeated in the case of each of the newspapers which
follow.

A very roughly printed newspaper with blurs and dis-
colorations wipes across and replaces its predecessor. The
newspaper marks a great deterioration in social efficiency.

It is printed from worn-out type and the lower lines
fall away.

THE WEEKLY PATRIOT

No. 1. New Series. February 2nd, 1952. *Price One Pound
Sterling.*

DRAWING TO THE END

"It is necessary to press on with the war with the utmost
determination. Only by doing so can we hope . . ."

A third paper wipes across this again:

THE WEEKLY PATRIOT

No. 754. March, 1955. *Price One Pound Sterling.*

THE UTMOST RESOLUTION. NO SURRENDER

A desolate heath. Something burning far away. A sheet
of decaying newspaper is fluttering in the wind. It catches
on a thorn and as the wind tears at it the audience has time
to read the ill-printed sheet of coarse paper:

BRITONS BULLETIN

September 21st, 1966. *Price Four Pounds Sterling.*

"Hold on. Victory is coming. The enemy is near the
breaking point . . ."

The wind tears the scrap of paper to pieces.

Here follows some still and desolate scene to suggest and symbolise our contemporary civilisation shattered to its foundations. The exact scene to be chosen could best be left to the imagination and invention and facilities of the model maker. It might even be different in the American, continental or British version of the film. *One* of the following scenes will give all the effects needed.

The Tower Bridge of London in ruins. No signs of human life. Sea gulls and crows. The Thames, partly blocked with debris, has overflowed its damaged banks.

The Eiffel Tower, prostrate. The same desolation and ruin.

Brooklyn Bridge destroyed. The tangle of cables in the water. Shipping sunk in the harbour. New York, ruined, in the background.

A sunken liner at the bottom of the sea.

A pleasure sea front, Palm Beach or the Lido, Blackpool or Coney Island, in complete and final ruin. A few wild dogs wander through the desolation.

Oxford University in ruins and the Bodleian Library scattered amidst the wreckage.

PART VIII

The Wandering Sickness

THE Central Square in Everytown. It is in ruins. A few ragged street vendors and a primitive market in a corner of the Square. A gigantic shell-hole is in the middle of the Square. A group of people stand about a board on the wall. This is a notice-board like the old Album on which news was written in the Roman Forum. As the world relapses old methods reappear.

Close shot of this group reading a smudgy cyclostyled notice on the board.

It reads:

NATIONAL BULLETIN

August   1968

WARNING!   A NEW OUTRAGE!

ENEMY SPREADING DISEASE BY AEROPLANE

"Our enemies, defeated on land and sea and in the air, have nevertheless retained a few aeroplanes which are difficult to locate and destroy. These they are using to spread disease, a new fever of mind and body. . . ."

Close up to emphasise date.

A man in a worn and patched uniform comes out of the Town Hall with a paper in his hand and turns towards the wall. A few people are attracted by his activity. He pastes up a new cyclostyled inscription.

The inscription, which runs a little askew, reads:

"The enemy are spreading the Wandering Sickness by aeroplane. Avoid sites where bombs have fallen. Do not drink stagnant water."

A woman comes out of a house. She is ragged and tired, a pail in her hand. She goes to the gigantic shell-hole in the middle of the Square. The woman descends with her pail. She wants some of the water. A man comes into the picture.

Man: "Didn't you read the warning?"

The woman answers with a tired mute "No."

Man, indicating the water: "Wandering Sickness."

The woman is struck by instant fear. Then she hesitates. "I have to go half an hour away for spring water."

The man shrugs his shoulders and goes. The woman is still hesitating.

The hospital under the laboratory. A dim dark place. The sick are unattended. One of them—a man in a dirty shirt and trousers—barefooted and haggard—rises, looks about him wildly and darts out.

The Square, outside the Hospital. The sick man wandering. He stares blankly in front of him. He seeks he knows not what. People in the Square see him and scatter. The woman in the shell-hole discovers the wandering sick man is approaching her. She screams and scrambles away. A group of men and women run away from the sick man.

A sentry with a rifle. A group of men and women enter the picture.

Man to sentry: "Don't you see?"

Woman: "He is carrying infection."

The sentry does not like his job, but he lifts his rifle. He fires. The wandering man collapses, writhes and lies still.

The sentry shouts: "Don't go near him. Leave him there!"

Dr. Harding's laboratory. Harding is at his work bench, assisted by his daughter, Mary. He is struggling desperately to work out the problem of immunity to the Wandering Sickness which is destroying mankind. He is now a man of fifty; he is overworked, jaded, aged. He is working in a partly wrecked laboratory with insufficient supplies. This laboratory has already been shown in the opening part. (The rooms downstairs have been improvised as a hospital, to which early cases of the pestilence are brought.) Harding's clothing is ragged and patched (no white overalls). His apparatus is more like an old alchemist's, it is makeshift and very inefficient. No power is laid on. There is no running water, though there is still a useless tap and a sink. But the brass microscopes are as before. They are difficult things to break. Bottles, crucibles, and such-like hardy stuff have survived, but very little fine glass. No Florence flasks, for example. Some old cans have been utilised. Several of the windows are cracked and have been mended with gummed paper.

Harding mutters as he works.

Mary is a girl of 18, dressed in a patched nurse's uniform, with a Red Cross armlet. "Father," she says, "why don't you sleep a little?"

Harding: "How can I sleep when my work may be the saving of countless lives?—countless lives!"

A shot is heard without. Harding goes to the window, followed by Mary.

Camera shooting from Harding's standpoint, showing the dead man with the Wandering Sickness, lying in his blood; Square deserted. A man walks across the scene, elaborately avoids the dead man, and puts a rag over his mouth to protect himself from infection.

Harding and Mary. Harding says: "And so our sanitation goes back to the cordon and killing! This is how they dealt with pestilence in the Dark Ages."

He makes a gesture of desperate impotence, shrugging his shoulders and throwing up his hands, and then turns back to his work-bench.

The room of Richard Gordon, a former air mechanic. It is like all the rooms of this period, shabby, with improvised or worn-out furniture. There is no proper tableware, only a sort of tramp's outfit of gallipots and tins. Richard's sister Janet is at a wood stove cooking a meal. Her movements are slow and spiritless. Richard Gordon, seated in front of an old table, is obviously waiting for the meal. He is deep in thought.

Instead of serving the meal Janet turns from the stove,

walks a few steps and then stares into space. Richard, roused from his thoughts, looks at her with growing terror and rises hurriedly. "What is it, Janet? Your heart?"

He takes her pulse. Deeply impressed: "I'll put you to bed, sister."

Janet sullenly silent. She shakes her head. Richard very tenderly tries to induce her to go to bed.

Return to Harding's laboratory. Harding at his microscope. Mary near him. Harding examines some preparation, and, without looking back, says: "Iodine, please."

Mary takes a step towards him. A glass or container in her hand. She looks at it and tilts it to ascertain its contents. She is unable to speak because she knows the portent of her answer.

Harding: "Mary!—iodine, please."

Mary: "There is no more, father. There is just one drop."

Harding turns back as if stabbed. "No more iodine?"

Mary replies with a shake of her head. Harding almost collapses and sits down. "My God!" He buries his head in his hands. His voice almost a sob: "What is the good of trying to save a mad world from its punishment?"

Mary: "Oh father, if you could only sleep for a time."

Harding: "How *can* I sleep? See how they wander out to die."

He rises and looks at his daughter, deeply moved: "And to think that I brought you into this world."

Mary: "Even now I am glad to be alive, father."

Harding pats her shoulder, a quick affectionate gesture. Then he walks up and down in deep mental distress.

"This is the last torment of this endless warfare. To know what life could do and be—and to be helpless."

He takes the slip from under the microscope eyepiece and dashes it to the floor in impotent rage.

He sits down in utter despair.

Mary makes futile movement to console him. A step on the staircase outside. They both look towards the door.

Mary: "Richard!"

Gordon enters. Harding stares at him, fearing his news.

Gordon : "My sister . . ."

Harding: "How—do you—know?"

Gordon: "Her heart beats fast. She feels faint. And—and —she won't answer."

Harding says nothing.

Gordon: "What can I do for her?"

Harding, pained, silent and beaten.

Gordon: "I thought—something—might be known."

Harding does not move. Mary cries: "Oh Janet!—and you, poor dear——"

She approaches Gordon and Gordon makes a movement as if to warn her that he too may be infected. She does not care. "Richard," she whispers, close to his face.

Harding rises and goes without a word. It is the doctor's instinct to try and help where everything seems hopeless.

Gordon's living-room. Janet turns to and fro on her bed. Enter Harding, followed by Richard and Mary. Harding approaches the bed. He pulls back the sheets, listens to Janet's breathing. Then he replaces the sheets and shakes his head. He rises from the bed. Gordon asks a mute question.

Harding: "No doubt of it. And it need not be. Oh to think of it! There is just one point still obscure. But I cannot even get iodine now—not even iodine! There is no more trade, nothing to be got. The war goes on. This pestilence goes on —unchallenged—worse than the wars that released it."

Gordon: "Is there nothing to make her comfortable?"

Harding: "Nothing. There is nothing to make anyone comfortable any more. War is the art of spreading wretchedness and misery. I remember when I was still a medical student, talking to a man named Cabal, about preventing war. And about the researches I would make and the ills I would cure. My God!"

Harding turns to the door and goes out.

The ruined and desolate Square as before. Harding crosses it, returning despairfully to his laboratory.

Gordon's living-room. Mary and Gordon sitting. Atmosphere of hopelessness. Both stare towards the bed. Janet rises. Her face is now ghastly white and her eyes are glassy. She comes towards the two and towards the audience. Mary and Gordon stare at her, horror-stricken, as she passes them. Her face advances to a close-up. She leaves the room. After a second's hesitation, Gordon rises and hurries after his sister. Mary takes a few steps and then sits down.

The Square. Janet wandering. Gordon reaches her and tries to take her arm, but she shakes him off. They go towards the crowd about the notice-board in front of the Town Hall. The crowd disperses, panic-stricken.

Janet and Gordon walking towards the sentry. The sentry lifts his rifle. Gordon protects Janet with his body. To sentry: "No! Don't shoot; I will take her out of the town."

Sentry hesitates. Janet wanders off the picture. Gordon hesitates between the sentry and her and then follows her. Sentry turns after them, still irresolute.

Janet and Gordon wander through the ruins of Everytown. She goes on ahead feverishly, aimlessly. He follows her. We are thus given a tour through Everytown in the uttermost phase of collapse. A dead city. Rats flee before them—starveling dogs.

They pass across a deserted railway station.

Public gardens in extreme neglect. Smashed notice-boards. Fountains destroyed—railings broken down.

Suburban road with villas empty and ruinous. In the gardens are bramble-thickets and nettle-beds. Janet and Gordon pass the former house of Passworthy, recognisable by the shattered fence.

Gradually the two figures, following each other, recede, and what follows is seen across wide desolate spaces at an increasing distance.

Janet drops and lies still. Gordon kneels down beside her.

At first he cannot believe she is dead. He picks her up in his arms and carries her off. He is seen far away carrying her into a mortuary.

Hooded figures come out to take her from him—all very far away.

Mary waiting in Gordon's room. It is now twilight and we see her face very sad and still and pale. She looks towards the door when at last Gordon comes staggering in. He is the picture of misery. "Oh Mary, dear Mary," he cries.

Mary holds out her arms to him. He clings to her like a child.

Three dates on the screen.

1968.

1969.

1970.

PART IX

Everytown under a Patriot Chief

THE Square of Everytown in 1970. It has a little recovered from the extreme tragic desolation of the Pestilence stage. Clumsy efforts to repair ruined buildings have been made. No shops have been reopened and half the houses are unoccupied, but the shell-hole in the centre has been filled up. There is a sort of market going on with patched and ragged people haggling for vegetables and bits of meat. Few people have boots. Most people are wearing footwear of bast and rags or sabots of wood. Few hats are worn and those old. The women are bareheaded or have shawls over their heads. The vehicles are *not* rude and primitive, but old broken-down stuff. One or two boxed things with old carriage wheels or motor car wheels—which people *push*. Few or no horses. A cow or a goat being milked. There is a peasant with a motor car (small runabout without tyres) with a lot of carrots and turnips in it, drawn by a horse. Several stalls are fairly full of second-hand stuff—clothing, furniture and household goods. It is like a small Caledonian Market. There is an old-clothes and miscellaneous stall with jewellery and worn-out finery. This is kept by an obsequious individual who might be an Oriental bazaar dealer. He rubs his hands and inspects another stall and watches the passers-by. No new stuff anywhere, because industrial life is at a standstill. The camera moves round to give a general view of the Square, coming to rest outside of the Town Hall. A big rosette flag hangs over the portico of the Town Hall. This rosette is the symbol of the ruling Boss and his government.

A small group watching a rosetted guard writing with charcoal on the wall!

At the top he has drawn and smeared a rough rosette.

NATIONAL BULLETIN
Mayday A.D. 1970

THE PESTILENCE HAS CEASED. Thanks to the determined action of our chief in shooting all wanderers. There have been no cases for two months. The Pestilence has been conquered.

THE CHIEF IS PREPARING TO RESUME HOSTILITIES AGAINST THE HILL PEOPLE WITH THE UTMOST VIGOUR. Soon we shall have Victory and Peace.

All is well—God save the Chief. God save our Land.

(Rosette)

Inside an aeroplane hangar. Gordon, three years older, and in a different, rather less dishevelled costume, is working on an aeroplane engine on the bench. Behind him is the dismantled aeroplane. Two assistants with him. He examines the high tension wires.

Gordon: "This rubber is perished. Have we any more insulated wire?"

First Assistant: "We've got no rubbered wire at all, sir."

Gordon: "Any rubber—tape?"

Second Assistant: "Not a scrap of rubber in the place. We used the last on the other motor."

Gordon slowly rises, defeated: "Oh, what's the use—there's no petrol anyway. I don't believe there's three gallons of petrol left in this accursed ruin of a town. What's the good of setting me at a job like this? Nothing will ever fly again. Flying is over. Everything is over. Civilisation is dead."

The Market. Camera swung round to the stall of gewgaws and old dresses. Roxana sailing down upon the trader. Roxana is a consciously beautiful young woman of eight and twenty. Her face is made up rather skilfully. In contrast to the dirty and dispirited people in the Square, she and her two attendant women seem brilliantly bright and prosperous. Her costume is best described as a collection of finery. It has been got together from the wardrobes and presses that are still to be found in the abandoned houses. It consists chiefly of an afternoon dress of *circa* 1935. Wadsky's stall is stocked with such findings.

Roxana, advancing: "Where is Wadsky? I want to speak to Wadsky."

Wadsky, who has been lurking behind his stall as she advances, pulls himself together and comes out to meet her.

Roxana: "You had a piece of flowered stuff, a whole length, seven yards, and you did not tell me of it. You kept it back from me, and you gave it to that woman of yours. And she's got a *new* dress—a *new* dress."

Wadsky disputes with his arms and shoulders while she speaks and when she pauses he says: "Ooh Lady, I showed you that piece."

Roxana: "Don't outface me, Wadsky. You have done that too often. You kept it from me!"

Wadsky: "Lady! You said: 'I don't want stuff like that.'"

Roxana: "Why! I had been asking for weeks for that very thing for the summer—light flowered cotton stuff."

Wadsky: "Oh, but Lady!"

Roxana: "How dared you? One would think I was of no importance in Everytown."

Roxana turns to her first attendant. "Don't you remember?—I *said* I wanted light stuff with flowers."

Attendant remembers dutifully.

D

Roxana appeals to her further. "What is the good of a Lover—what is the good of a powerful lover, if one is to be treated like this?"

Roxana to Wadsky, who is bowing, very disgruntled. "I'll tell the Chief. I've warned you before. Everything first to me."

Swing away from her to another part of the Market Square. A little excited knot has formed round a ragged man.

Man: "I saw it with my own eyes."

Crowd laughs.

Woman: "First you drink and then you see things."

Man: "First I heard the noise, then I looked up and there it was—far away up in the sky—over the hills."

Gordon is seen coming through the Square towards them. He hears the last remarks of the man. "What did you see?"

Man: "An aeroplane—flying away there over the hills. Just about dawn it was."

The crowd jeers at him. Gordon looks at the man, sums him up, shrugs his shoulders, and goes on his way.

Mary is buying vegetables from the peasant with the horse-drawn car. She is dressed in a rough simple costume of brownish stuff. But it suits her style. Gordon appears and they greet one another with the casualness of married people. While Mary selects food, Gordon looks at the car with professional affection. "It's a Morris, isn't it?"

Peasant: "Yes—a good pre-pestilence machine. I oil it and turn it over at times."

Gordon: "You think it might go fast some day? Still?"

Peasant: "Say! I'm not one of those petrol hoarders. But all the same that engine turns over still. Why I remember when I was a boy—when it was new—we thought nothing of going a hundred miles in it—a whole hundred miles. Less than three hours I've done it in. But all that sort of thing has gone—gone for ever! Eh?"

He looks with a sort of sceptical cunning inquiry at Gordon.

Gordon and Mary finish their purchases and go towards the laboratory.

Mary: "You are late to-day. Did you get anything done?"

Gordon: "Nothing. The machines are rotten. There's no petrol. It's mockery for the Boss to set me at it. We'll never get one of them up. Flying has become a dream for Bosses and such-like drunken men. There was a drunken man over there, by the by, swearing he *saw* an aeroplane this morning."

Mary: "Richard!"

Gordon: "What is it?"

Mary: "You won't think me mad?"

Gordon: "Eh?"

Mary: "*I* heard an aeroplane this morning."

Gordon: "When?"

Mary: "At dawn. I thought it was a dream. But if some-one else——"

Gordon: "Nonsense. I tell you flying is finished. We shall never get in the air again. Never."

Fifes and drums are heard. They turn abruptly, with a certain uneasiness of bearing.

The Boss with his retinue. They are a semi-military brigand crew with little that is uniform about them except the prevalent rosette badges. They march through the Square. The Boss is a big swaggering fellow with a hat cocked on one side bearing a rosette in front of it. His frogged tunic might have belonged to a guards' bandsman. He has a sword, a dirk and two pistols. Neat riding breeches and boots. A scarf tied across his breast bears the rosette symbol. His manners might be described as the decaying civilities of a London taxi-cab driver. His underlings have compiled quasi-military costumes similar to his own.

He recognises Gordon, glances at Mary, betrays a momentary appreciation, decides to show off at her and halts. Gordon makes a half-hearted salute.

Boss: "Anything to report, Gordon?"

Gordon: "Nothing very hopeful, Chief."

Boss: "We must have those planes—somehow."

Gordon: "I'll do what I can, but you can't fly without petrol."

Boss: "I'll get petrol for you, trust *me*. *You* see to the engines. I know you haven't got stuff—but surely you can get round that. For example, transfer parts. Have you tried that? Use bits of one to mend the other. Be resourceful. Give me only ten in working order. Give me only five. I don't want them all. I'll see to it you get your reward. Then we can end this war of ours—for good. This your wife, Gordon? You've kept her hidden. Salutation, lady! You must use your influence with our Master Mechanic, lady. The combatant State needs his work."

Mary doesn't like the situation. "I'm sure my husband does his best for you, Chief."

Boss: "His *best!* That isn't enough, lady. The combatant State demands miracles."

Mary pauses and then speaks rather stupidly: "It isn't everyone, Chief, who can work miracles—as you do."

Boss, most elated: "I am sure *you* could work miracles, lady, if you choose."

The voice of Roxana heard off. "Rudolf!"

The manner of the Boss becomes slightly deflated. He turns towards Roxana who approaches rustling with indignation, followed by her three ladies-in-waiting. Gordon and Mary are ignored forthwith. Behind, in a state of nervous apprehension, hovers Wadsky.

Roxana: "Here they are at their old tricks! Wadsky has been keeping things back from me! Is that with your permission?"

Wadsky: "But she was shown it. She said she didn't want it."

Boss: "If Wadsky has been at his old tricks again he must answer for them."

Roxana turns triumphantly towards Wadsky.

Boss: "It isn't only Wadsky who keeps things back. What do you think of our Master Mechanic here—who won't give me planes to finish up that little war of ours with the Hill People."

Roxana surveys Gordon with her arms akimbo, and then considers Mary and the Boss more deliberately. She rather likes the look of Gordon. She perceives that the Boss has been showing off at Mary and she wants to take him down a little.

She speaks with a faint shrewish mockery to the Boss. "Can't you *make* him? I thought you could make everybody do everything."

Gordon: "Some things can't be done, Madam. You can't fly without petrol. You can't mend machines without tools or material. We've gone back too far. Flying is a lost skill in Everytown."

Roxana: "And are you really as stupid as *that?*"

Gordon: "I'm as helpless as that."

Roxana to the Boss: "And now Chief—what are you going to do about it?"

Boss, becoming the strong man: "He's going to put those machines in order and I'm going to find him—coal—stuff to make his oil."

The throbbing of an aeroplane very far away becomes faintly audible. Close-up of Gordon's face.

Gordon: "It's a lost skill. It is a dream of the past."

His face changes as the beating of the aeroplane dawns on his consciousness. He is puzzled. Then his face changes. He looks up in the sky. He points silently.

The whole group is shown. All are staring upward.

Wadsky and the market people, the general crowd in the background, are all becoming aware of the aeroplane. The aeroplane is seen circling in the sky. This has to be the first *novel* aeroplane seen in the film. It is to be a small new 1970 type. Its wings curve back like a swallow's. It must not be big and impressive like the gas bomber which presently arrives, but it must be "different."

People run out of houses. Everybody staring skywards. Running, shouting—the excitement grows.

Gordon, deeply moved. He addresses Mary. "There it is— you were right—a plane once more! He's shutting off—he's coming down."

The eye of the crowd follows the plane and indicates it is circling down to a descent.

The Boss is the first to become active. "What's all this? Have they got aeroplanes before us? And you tell me we can't fly any more! While we have been—fumbling, they have been active. Here, some of you, find out who this is and what it means! *You* (to one of his guards), you go, and *you* (to another). There was only one man in it. Hold him."

The Boss is a centre of activity.

Boss: "Send for Simon Burton. Get me Simon."

A sly-looking individual, the right-hand man of the Boss, appears from the direction of the Town Hall and hurries up to his chief.

The camera shows Gordon and Mary standing a little aloof, perplexed, full of strange hope, at this wonderful break in the routines of Everytown. Then it returns to Roxana. She watches the Boss and his proceedings with the sceptical criticism of a woman who knows a man too well. Then her mind returns to Mary and she looks for her and discovers Gordon also. She comes across to them.

Roxana to Gordon: "What do you know about it? Do you know anything of this? Who is that man in the air?"

Gordon speaks half to himself and half to Roxana and Mary. "It was something *new*. It was a *new* machine. Somewhere they can still make new machines. I didn't dream it was still possible."

Roxana: "But *who* is the man? How does he *dare* come here?"

Close-up of her face as she surveys Everytown and realises that after all it is not the whole world. Her eyes return to the Boss who is still rather uncertain how to meet this new occasion.

Boss: "Fetch him to the Town Hall. Guard his machine and bring him to me there."

The camera returns to Gordon and Mary.

Gordon: "Come along, Mary. I must see that machine."

A field close to the town. People running. The aeroplane glides overhead and lands just out of sight over the brow of a slight hill.

A few ragged men, women and children run up so as to stand out against the sky and look. They hesitate and keep their distance. A child starts forward but his mother stops him—they stare, and they begin to move uneasily right and left from the centre of the ridge as something unseen approaches. The two guards sent by the Boss appear and hesitate.

We are looking towards the aeroplane across a hollow so that with quite dramatic suddenness John Cabal, the airman, the father of the children in the opening part, rises above the crest and comes towards us.

He is now grey-haired with a lined face. He is dressed in shiny black and he wears a sort of circular shield over head and body that makes him over seven feet high. It is like a round helmet enclosing body as well as head. It is a 1970 gas mask. The vizor in front swings *down*, so that his head and shoulders seen from in front are suggestive of a Buddha against a circular halo. The black mask behind his head and shoulders is ribbed like a scallop shell. He stands out against the sky, a tall portent. He walks through the watchers who follow him—one guard goes over the crest towards the machine, the other guard approaches him. This second guard and Cabal go towards the town. This second guard is an oafish unshaven creature, greatly puzzled by life at all times and excessively puzzled now. A group of curious men and women follow them.

Cabal: "Who's in control of this part of the country?"

Guard: "The chief. What we call the Boss."

Cabal: "Good. I want to see him!"

Guard: "He sent me to arrest you."

Cabal: "Well—you can't. But I'll come and see him."

Guard: "Well, you're under arrest—whether you admit it or not. This country is at war."

The crowd and particularly various children come closer to Cabal.

Cabal: "I remember this place well. I lived oh—somewhere down there." (Points.) "For years. Ever heard of a man called Passworthy? Any of you? No! Harding?"

Two children speak together. "Doctor Harding!"

Cabal: "Yes, is *he* still here?"

Old Woman: "He's a good man. He's our only doctor here. Oh, he's a good man."

Children: "Look, here he is, sir!"

Harding, Gordon and Mary seen approaching. Crowd in background.

Cabal and Harding scrutinise each other.

Cabal: "Heavens! Is that *Harding?*"

Harding, perplexed: "I seem to remember something—something about you."

Cabal: "But you were a *young* man!"

Harding cries out: "You are *John Cabal!* I used to come to your house! *Here!* Endless years ago. Before the wars began. And you are flying! You are grey but you look—young still!"

Cabal: "How are things in this place? Who's in control?"

Harding looks discreetly at crowd: "We've got a chief here —a war lord. The usual thing."

Cabal takes Harding by the arm: "H'm. I've come to look up your war lord. Where can we go to talk?"

Harding gesticulates to indicate where he lives. Cabal makes to go with him.

Guard: "Here! You're under arrest, you know. You've got to come to the chief."

Cabal: "All in good time. This gentleman first."

Guard: "You can't do that. You've got to come with me. Orders are orders. The Boss first."

Cabal lifts his eyebrows and goes off with Harding. Guard following with gestures of amazement and protest. "Here. Here. Here," he says. Then come Gordon and Mary and the rabble. The rabble is astonished at Cabal's cavalier treatment of the guard.

In the laboratory. Remains of a meal. The meal has been a squalid one. Cans—only a knife or so and a broken fork. No cloth, cracked bowls. Mary, Gordon, Cabal and Harding in conversation. Cabal has removed his great body gas-mask and swings it beside him.

The guard opens the door and looks in.

Cabal: "You keep out. I shall be all right here."

The guard seems about to speak and then catches Cabal's eye and shuts the door again.

Cabal: "And so you came back here after the war?"

Harding: "And became a sort of medieval leech. A doctor without medicines or instruments. I do what I can in this broken down world. Good heavens! Do you remember how I used to blow about the research I was going to do?"

Cabal comes and sits down: "*Don't* I remember? You had some good ideas. But look here—tell me things. How are things here? Are there any mechanics left? Any capable technical workers?"

Harding: "This is the very man."

Gordon comes forward and Cabal scrutinises him. "What are you?"

Gordon: "Ex-air-mechanic, sir. Jack of all trades now. The last engineer in Everytown."

Cabal: "Pilot?"

Gordon: "Yes, sir." (Salutes.) "Not so very skilful. I wish I was a better mechanic."

The guard opens the door again and peeps in. "My orders," he begins.

Cabal: "Never mind your orders. *Shut—that—door.*" The guard obeys.

Cabal: "Tell me about this Boss you have here. What sort of man has got hold of this part of the world?"

The Boss's headquarters in the Town Hall. He has staged things for the reception of the strange airman. He sits at a vast desk. A few guards, secretaries and yes-men around him. Simon Burton sits at a side table. Roxana watches proceedings—comes and stands close beside the Boss at his right hand. Whispers to him. She displays the excitement of a woman before a bull fight. A lively contest is going to happen and she has an impression that the strange visitant may prove an interesting novelty. Things have been dull in Everytown lately.

The atmosphere is strained. The scene is set and the principal actor does not enter. The Boss is impatient to see Cabal and Cabal does not come. Messengers are sent and return.

Boss: "Where is this man? Why isn't he brought here?"

Everyone looks uneasy. The Boss turns to Burton.

Burton: "He has gone off with Doctor Harding."

The Boss rises. "He *has* to be brought here. I must deal with him."

Roxana lays a hand on his arm. "But you can't go to him. That's impossible. He must come to you."

The Boss hesitates and sits restless under her dominance.

"Send another man for him. Send three men. With clubs. He must be brought here at once."

Burton hurries out to give the order.

The laboratory. The group talking.

Cabal: "So that's the sort of man your Boss is. Not an unusual type. Everywhere, you see, we find these little semi-military upstarts robbing, fighting. That is what endless warfare has worked out to—brigandage. What else could happen? And we, who are all that is left of the old engineers and mechanics, are turning our hands to salvage the world. We have the air-ways, what is left of them, we have the sea. We have ideas in common; the freemasonry of efficiency—the brotherhood of science. We are the natural trustees of civilisation when everything else has failed."

Gordon: "Oh, I have been waiting for this. I am yours to command."

Cabal: "Not mine. Not mine. No more bosses. Civilisation's to command. Give yourself to World Communications."

A knock at the door. They turn. The oafish guard comes into the room. Three others who have been sent for him by the Boss are behind. One of them says: "Tell him he's got to come. If he won't come on his feet, we'll carry him."

The First Guard: "Lord knows what will happen to me, sir, if you do not come."

Cabal shrugs his shoulders, rises, reflects, hands his great gas-mask to Gordon and stalks out, the guards following respectfully.

The gas-mask is not in evidence in the next scene.

The Town Hall. The Boss at his great desk. Roxana very alert behind him. Simon Burton at his own table. As the guard and Cabal approach, the Boss draws himself up in his chair, and attempts a lordly pose. Cabal's bearing is easy and familiar. The Boss is sturdy and ornate. Cabal tall, lean, black and dry.

Cabal: "Well, what do you want to talk to me about?"

Boss: "Who are you? Don't you know this country is at war?"

Cabal: "Dear, dear! Still at it. We must clean that up."

Boss: "What do you mean? We must clean that up? War is war. Who are *you*, I say?"

Cabal pauses before he replies. "The law," he says.

He improves it: "Law and sanity."

Roxana watches him. Then looks to the Boss.

Boss, a little late: "*I* am the law here."

Cabal: "I said law and sanity."

Boss: "Where do you come from? What are you?"

Cabal: "Pax Mundi. Wings over the world."

Boss: "Well, you know, you can't come into a country at war in this fashion."

Cabal: "I'm here. Do you mind if I sit down."

He sits down and leans across the table looking intelligently and familiarly into the face of the Boss.

"Well?" he says.

Boss: "And now for the fourth time who are you?"

Cabal: "I tell you Wings—Wings over the World."

Boss: "That's nothing. What Government are you under?"

Cabal: "Commonsense. Call us Airmen if you like. We just run ourselves."

Boss: "You'll run into trouble if you land here in war time. What's the game?"

Cabal: "Order and trade——"

Boss: "Trade, eh? Can you do anything in munitions?"

Cabal: "Not our line of business."

Boss: "Petrol—spare parts? We've got planes—we've got planes—we've got boys who've trained a bit on the ground. But we've got no fuel. It hampers us. We might do a deal."

Cabal reflects and looks at his toes: "We might."

Boss: "I know where I can get some fuel. Later. I've got my plans. But if you could manage a temporary accommodation—we'd do business."

Cabal: "Airmen help no one to make war."

Boss, impatiently: "End war, I said. End war. We want to make a victorious peace."

Cabal: "I seem to have heard that phrase before. When I was a young man. But it made no end to war."

Boss: "Now look here, Mr. Aviator. Let's be clear how things are. Come down to actuality. The way you swagger there, you don't seem to understand you are under arrest. You and your machine."

Mutual mute interrogation.

Cabal: "You'll get other machines looking for me—if I happen to be delayed."

Boss: "We'll deal with them later. You can start a trading agency here if you like. *I've* no objection. And the first thing we shall want will be to have our own aeroplanes in the air again."

He looks for confirmation to Burton, who nods approval and then to Roxana. But Roxana is staring at Cabal to hear his next words.

Cabal: "Yes. An excellent ambition. But our new order has an objection to private aeroplanes."

Roxana, softly for Boss to hear: "The *impudence!*"

Boss half glances at her with a faint anxiety. She has sometimes the habit of taking the word in discussions. "I am not talking of *private* aeroplanes. The aeroplanes we have here are the public aeroplanes of our combatant State. This is a free and sovereign State. At war. I don't know anything about any new order. I am the chief here, and I am not going to take any orders—old or new, from you."

Cabal leans back in his chair and reflects. He says, with a faint gleam of amusement: "I suppose I have walked into trouble."

Boss: "You may take that as right."

Simon Burton is about to say something, and then thinks better of it. Roxana is more outspoken: "Where do you come from?"

Cabal smiles and addresses himself deliberately to her: "I flew from our headquarters at Basra yesterday. I spent the night at an old aerodrome at Marseilles. We are gradually restoring order and trade all over the Mediterranean. We have some hundreds of aeroplanes and we are making more, fast. We have factories at work again. I'm just scouting a bit to see how things are here."

Boss: "And you've found out. We've got order here, the old order, and we don't want anybody else restoring it, thank you. This is an independent combatant State."

Cabal: "We've got to talk about that."

Boss: "We don't discuss it."

Cabal: "We don't approve of these independent combatant States."

Boss: "You don't approve."

Cabal: "*We* mean to stop them."

Boss: "That's—war."

Cabal: "As you will. My people know I'm prospecting. When they find I don't come back they'll send a force to look for me."

Boss, grimly: "Perhaps they won't find you."

Cabal shrugs his shoulders. "They'll find *you*."

Boss: "They'll find me *ready*. Well, I think we know now where we stand. You four guards take this man, and if he gives any trouble, club him. *Club* him. You hear that, Mr. Wings over your Wits? See to it, Burton. Have him taken to the detention room downstairs."

He stands up as if dismissing the assembly.

The Camera goes to a smaller apartment behind the large room of the previous scene. It is the Boss's retiring room. Roxana enters first and turns to the Boss who is following her.

Roxana, exasperatingly critical: "Now was that *wise?*"

Boss, irritated at once: "*Wise!*"

Roxana: "Yes, wise; was it wise to quarrel with him at once?"

Boss: "Quarrel with him! Confound him, he began to quarrel with me!—'We must clean that up!'—Clean that up! *My* war!"

Roxana: "But—but there's things behind him."

Boss: "Things behind him! Some sort of air bus driver. Standing up to *me*—like an equal."

Roxana: "So you lost your temper and bullied him."

Boss: "I didn't bully. I just took the fellow in hand."

Roxana: "No, Rudolf. You bully. And you bully too soon."

Boss: "I don't seem able to please you to-day."

Roxana: "Well, if you must go from one tactless thing to another. Weakening your authority. Sacrificing dignity."

Boss: "Here! What's the *matter* with you?"

Roxana: "Oh, *I* saw! There's your head mechanic—an essential man for your work—and you can't keep your eyes off his wife! Don't I *know* you. But never mind that. I've learnt to overlook that sort of thing. What I ask again—whether you bully me or not—is, whether it was wise to take this man in this way?"

Boss: "How else could he be taken? How else?"

Roxana: "Well, look at it! This is the first *real* aviator that has come our way for years. Think of what that means, my dear! You want aeroplanes, don't you? You want your aeroplanes put in order? Well—I've always doubted if that young man Gordon was up to the job. He's good-looking in a weak sort of way—but is he really skilful and scientific? He—fumbles. He just goes about with this girl of his—whom you think so good-looking. A really *clever* man would have had some of those machines up long ago. I'm sure of it."

Boss: "So along comes this stranger who is going to *clean me up*. And you propose I shall hand over my aeroplanes to him, lock, stock and barrel."

Roxana: "Why talk nonsense? You could have persuaded him—under supervision."

Boss: "Supervision. The sort of oafs I have here to supervise him. He'd be too much for them."

Roxana: "If he's going to be too much for you, hang him and hide his machine before the others get after you. But if he *isn't* going to be too much for you——"

Boss: "He's *not* going to be too much for me."

Roxana: "Very well. The hand of iron in the glove of velvet. Where is the benefit in abusing him and locking him up?"

Boss: "I don't agree with you. I don't agree with you. Oh, I don't agree with you. Now listen. Listen to me. You don't understand. *Now is our time.* You think I'm a fool. But let me tell you one or two things I've had in mind. If you watched my mind a little more and my movements a little less it might be better for you."

Simon Burton joins them unobtrusively and listens deferentially.

Boss: "This—this stranger—hasn't taken me by surprise. I knew this thing was coming."

Close up of incredulous faces of Roxana and Simon Burton.

Boss: "Yes, I knew this was coming. I *felt* they'd got ahead with their air force down there. I *felt* there was this conspiracy of air bus drivers brewing somewhere in the world. Very well. Now's the time. We've got this fellow bottled up for a week or so. They may not begin to miss him for days. I've got everything fixed now for an attack straight away up the Floss Valley to the old coal and shale pits—where there's oil too! And then—up we buzz. Wings over the Hill-State. Everybody has laughed at my air force that never even crawls on the ground. But they won't laugh then."

Roxana: "My dear, that's all right. But it doesn't explain why you treat that new man as an enemy. I don't believe Gordon is a good mechanic. But evidently *he* is."

Boss: "Don't *harp* on that! You always think you know better than I do—about everything."

Roxana slowly: "I'm going to talk to this man myself."

Boss: "If *that* sort of thing is what you were after——!"

Roxana: "Oh, you don't understand."

Boss: "Don't understand! You spare neither youth nor age. You leave that man to me. You leave that fellow **alone.**"

Scene changes to a small bare room like the waiting-room of a police station. It is poorly lit by a barred window. Cabal sits on a wooden chair with his arms on a bare table and contemplates the situation.

Cabal: "I've tumbled into a hole. It's the old old story of the over confident wise man and the truculent rough. . . . It may be weeks before I'm reported as missing. They'll think my radio has broken down. Meanwhile Mr. Boss here does as he likes. . . ."

"Escape?"

He contemplates the room. Stands up and stares at the window bars.

"They'll have my machine guarded. . . ."

Sits down again, laughs bitterly at himself and drums with his fingers on the table exactly as he did in Part III of the film.

Then he jumps up impatiently. Goes to the window. Close up of his face in the dim light.

"I suppose everyone must do something hopelessly foolish at times. I've walked into it. I—the planner of a new world. . . .

"Just at this time with everything ready. . . .

"If this mad war dog here bites me—and I die—I wonder who will carry on. . . .

"No man is indispensable . . ."

He tries the firmness of the bars in the window. Fade out upon his hands holding the bars.

Scene outside the Town Hall.   A small troop of mounted men with a flag leaving for the war. Two led horses are brought up and the Boss and Roxana appear and mount.

The whole body rides off.

A small not very enthusiastic crowd watches their departure. There is a feeble cheer as the detachment goes off.

Fight on a hill overlooking coal pits. The Boss directs operations. With him are his irregular troop leaders. They gallop off.

The coal pits. The Boss's cavalry attack some rough trenches. The defenders are overwhelmed and seen running away. One or two flashes of the little battle. The Boss's men are plainly victorious, the enemy routed.

The Central Square. A troop of mounted men ride into the

Square. Following comes the Boss and Roxana triumphant. Flags decorate the side streets. The crowd shows a new enthusiasm. People cheer as the Boss and Roxana pull up outside the Town Hall.

Close up of a group of lookers-on. One man is explaining to another:

Man: "We have captured the coal pits, and the old oil retorts, and we have got oil at last."

Close up of a lean, excited patriotic youngster wearing a rosette badge. "Now we'll bomb the hills to hell."

In the Town Hall. A day later. The Boss still flushed with triumph. Most of his usual entourage is present, but Roxana is not there at first. Eight or nine officers of the little army are present. Gordon is seen under arrest near the Boss's desk. The Boss walks up and down and orates:

Boss: "Victory approaches. Your sacrifices have not been in vain. Our long struggle with the Hill Men has come to its climax. Our victory at the old coal pits has brought a new supply of oil within reach. Once more we can hope to take the air and look invaders in the face. We have nearly forty aeroplanes, as big a force, I venture to say, as any in the world now. This oil we have got can be adapted to our engines. That is quite a simple business. Nothing remains to be done but a conclusive bombing of the hills. Then for a time we shall have a rich and rewarding peace, the peace of the strong man armed who keepeth his house. And now at this supreme crisis you, Gordon, our master engineer, must needs refuse to help us. Where are my planes?"

Gordon: "The job is more difficult than you think. Half your machines are hopelessly old. You haven't got twenty sound ones. To be exact, nineteen. You'll never get the others off the ground. The thing cannot be done as you imagine it. I want assistance."

Boss: "What assistance?"

Gordon: "Your prisoner."

Boss turns to him. "You want that fellow in black—Wings over the World? You want him released?"

Gordon: "He knows his business. I don't enough. Make him my—technical adviser."

Boss: "I don't trust you technical fellows."

Gordon: "Then you won't get an aeroplane up."

Boss: "I want those planes."

Gordon shrugs his shoulders.

The Boss meditates, walking to and fro.

Boss: "And if you get him?"

Gordon: "Then I want Doctor Harding out too."

Boss: "They're—old associates."

Gordon: "I can't help that. If anybody in Everytown can adapt that crude oil for our aeroplanes it is Harding. If not, it can't be done."

Boss: "We've had a bit of an argument with Harding."

Gordon: "He's the only man who can do this work for you."

Boss: "Bring in Harding."

Enter Roxana with a certain quiet dignity while the assembly awaits Harding. The Boss glances at her as if he would rather she had not come. She stands regarding the scene critically.

Harding is brought in. He is dishevelled, and his hands are tied. He looks as if he had been manhandled.

Boss: "Untie his hands."

The guard releases Harding.

The Boss pauses and looks at Harding. "Well?"

Harding: "Well, what?"

Boss: "The salute."

Harding: "Damn the salute."

The guard steps forward to strike Harding, but Roxana intervenes.

Roxana : "No."

Boss: "Never mind the salute now. We'll talk about that afterwards. Now let us see where we are. You, Gordon, are to direct the reconstruction of our air forces. The prisoner Cabal is to be put at your disposal. Everywhere he goes he is to be under guard and observation. No relaxing on that. And neither he nor you must go within fifty yards of his plane. Mind *that!* You, Harding, are to help Gordon with this fuel problem and to put your knowledge of poison gas at our disposal."

Harding: "I tell you, I will do nothing with poison gas."

Boss: "You've got the knowledge—if I have to wring it out of you. The Combatant State is your father and your mother, your only protector, the totality of your interests. No discipline can be stern enough for the man who denies that by word or deed."

Harding: "Nonsense. We have our duty to civilisation. You and your like are heading back to eternal barbarism."

The entourage is dumbfounded. Burton starts forward. "But this is pure treason."

Harding: "In the name of civilisation, I protest against being dragged from my work. Confound your silly wars! Your war material and all the rest of it! All my life has been interrupted and wasted and spoilt by war. I will stand it no more."

Burton: "This is Treason—Treason."

Guards rush upon Harding, seize him and twist his arms. Harding snarls with pain. Roxana comes forward.

Roxana: "No. Stop that."

The guards stop. Harding is sullen and silent. Boss comes very close to him.

Boss: "We have need of your services."

Harding: "Well, what do you want?"

Boss: "You are conscripted. You are under my orders now and under no others in the world. I am the master here! I am the State. I want fuel—and gas."

Harding: "Neither fuel nor gas."

Boss: "You refuse?"

Harding: "Absolutely."

Boss: "I do not want to be forced to extremities."

Roxana is whispering to the Boss, with her eyes on Gordon. Gordon comes fully into the picture. He has a scheme of his own. He looks hard at Roxana as though he was silently trying to will her aid. The confidence in his manner, the faint streak of impudence in his nature, increases.

Gordon: "Sir—may I have a word? I understand you want all of these out-of-date crocks of yours which you call your air force, to fly again—and fly well?"

Boss: "They *shall*."

Gordon: "With the help of that man—Cabal—you have in the cells here, and with the help of Doctor Harding here —you may even get a dozen of your planes in the air again."

Harding: "You are a traitor to civilisation. I won't touch it."

Gordon ignores him: "If you will give me Cabal and— if you will leave me free to talk with the Doctor, I promise you will see your air force—a third of it at any rate—in the sky again."

Boss: "You talk as though you were driving a bargain with me."

Gordon: "I am sorry, Chief. It is not I who make these conditions. It is in the nature of things. You cannot have technical services, you cannot have scientific help unless you treat the men who give it you—properly."

Roxana to the Boss, but quite loud: "That's what I have said all along! You are bullying too much, my dear. There is a limit to bullying. Why! you can't make a *dog* hunt by beating it."

Boss: "I want those aeroplanes."

Gordon: "Well."

Boss: "And I mean to be master here."

Roxana: "Then you have to be reasonable, my dear, and that's all about it."

Close up of the Boss wondering where Mastery ends and Reasonableness begins.

Gordon and Cabal at work upon that aeroplane engine which was puzzling Gordon at the opening of this part. The two men quite understand each other. Cabal works and Gordon learns from him. The four guards watch and poke their noses about and listen conscientiously but perplexedly. They glance at one another. They are much too oafish to control the conversation.

Cabal between his teeth: "If only they'd let us go back to my own plane. There's a radio there."

Gordon: "Hopeless. . . . Won't even trust me."

Cabal: "We'll have to make a job of this."

Gordon: "I could send men for your reserve petrol. They'll give me that. For this."

Cabal: "Good." Then louder as if explaining the machine. "One of the most difficult bits in this is what is called the get-a-way—it's a sort of cut-out. But I have some ideas."

Gordon: "We'll manage it I think. Now that Dr. Harding understands his part of the job. . . ."

They nod reassuringly to each other and then glance at the stupid faces of their guards. It's safe.

Evening. Cabal is sitting in his cell lit by the light of two candles. He looks bored and despondent. He turns round at a knocking at his door. "Come in. Don't stand on ceremony." The door is opened deferentially by a guard. Roxana appears, rather specially dressed. Cabal has not expected anything of this sort. He is a man of experience with women although he has none of the Boss's devouring enterprise. He stands up. She walks in, carrying herself with a certain consciousness of her effect. He bows and remains silent.

Roxana: "I wanted to look at you."

Cabal stiffly: "At your service, Madam."

Roxana: "You are the most interesting thing that has happened in Everytown for years."

Cabal: "You honour me."

Roxana: "You come from—outside. I had begun to forget there was anything outside. I want to hear about it."

Cabal: "May I offer you my only chair?"

Roxana sits down and arranges herself. Then she takes a look at Cabal to gauge her effect. Cabal stands or leans against the table in the subsequent conversation. He looks at her only very occasionally, but they are scrutinizing glances.

Roxana: "You know—I am not a stupid woman."

Cabal: "I am sure."

Roxana: "This life here—is limited. War—rich plunder. Shining prizes. Of a sort. War always going on and never ending. Flags. Marching. I adore the Chief. I've always adored him since he took control in the Pestilence Days when everyone else lost heart. He rules. He is firm. Everyone— every woman finds him strong and attractive. I can't complain. I have everything that is to be had here. But——"

Cabal looks at her for a moment. What is she up to? He makes a faint encouraging noise: "M'm."

Roxana: "This is a small limited world we live in here. *You* bring in the breath of something greater. When I saw you swooping down out of the sky—when I saw you march into the Town Hall—I felt: this man lives in a greater world. And you spoke of the Mediterranean and the East, and your camps and factories. I've read about the Mediterranean and Greece and Egypt and India. I can read—a lot of those old books. I'm not like most of the younger people. I learnt a lot before education stopped and the schools closed down. I want to see that world away there. Sunshine, palms, snowy mountains, blue seas."

Cabal: "If I had my way—you might fly to all that in a couple of days."

Roxana becomes pensive and looks down: "If you were free. . . . And if I was free."

Cabal's expression reveals a flash of curiosity about her. "What *is* she up to?"

Roxana: "I don't think any man has ever understood any woman since the beginning of things. You don't understand our imaginations. How wild our imaginations can be."

Cabal decides he will not interrupt her.

Roxana: "I wish I were a man."

She stands up abruptly. "Oh if I were a man! . . . Does any man realise what the life of a woman is? How trivial we *have* to be. We have to please. We are obliged to please. If we attempt to take a serious share in life, are we welcomed? And all the while—— Men are so self-satisfied, so blind, so limited. . . . I see things happening here——! Injustice. Cruelty. There are things I would do for the poor—things I would do to make things better. I am not allowed. I have to pretend to be eaten up by my dresses, my jewels, my

vanities. I make myself beautiful often with an aching heart.
. . . But I'm talking about myself. Tell me about yourself—
about that greater world you live in. Are *you* a Boss? You
have the manner of one who commands. You are sure of
yourself. You make me afraid of you. Of the people you
come from. Of what you are. Before you came I felt safe here.
I felt—things were going on as they have been going on. . . .
Always. . . . No hope of change. . . . *Now*—it's all different.
What are you people trying to do to us? What do you mean
to do to this Boss of mine?"

Cabal: "Well, the immediate question seems to be what
does he mean to do to me?"

Roxana: "Something foolish and violent—unless I prevent
it."

Cabal: "That is how I see things."

Roxana: "If he kills you——?"

Cabal: "We shall come here and clean things up just the
same."

Roxana: "But if you are killed—how can you say *we*?"

Cabal: "Oh, *we* go on. That's just how it is, *we* are taking
hold of things. In science and government—in the long run—
no man is indispensable. The human thing goes on. *We*—for
ever."

Roxana: "I see. And our Combatant State here?"

Cabal: "Has to vanish into the shadows. After the
Tyrannosaurus and the sabre-toothed tiger."

Roxana stands looking at him. He leans against the table
and smiles at her.

Roxana: "You are a new sort of man to me."

Cabal: "No. A new sort of training. The old Adam
fundamentally."

She goes off at a tangent again. "I suppose at the bottom
of her heart every woman despises a man she can manage.

And all women despise men who run after women. . . . "

Cabal: "You're not by any chance thinking of the Chief? Where is he to-night?"

Roxana: "Drinking and boasting. And after that, he hopes to betray me without my finding out. Vain hopes, I'm afraid. We needn't think about him. If I said I still love him, it is as one loves a dirty troublesome child. I love him and he doesn't matter. What I am thinking about is *you*. And this new world of yours—oh, it's *your* world—that I can feel advancing on us."

Pause.

Cabal: "Well?"

Roxana: "Have men of your sort no use for women?"

Cabal: "Madam, I'm a widower and a grandfather. I see these things with a philosophical detachment. And I don't quite know what you mean by *use*."

Roxana: "A man is a man till he's dead. Don't you still want the help of a woman? Have you no use for that closeness of devotion you can never get from any man? Don't you see I have been working for you already? See what I have done for you! I have saved Harding from ill-treatment. I got you half released so as to work with Gordon. I may be able at last to release you altogether. Why do you despise me?"

Cabal: "I don't despise you in the least. I think you are the most *civilised* being I have met yet in Everytown."

Roxana: "More than your friends?"

Cabal: "Oh, *much* more."

Roxana is pleased. She presses on to her next step. "Why don't you confide in *me*? There's Gordon, there's his wife Mary and her father Harding, and you are all—*together*, in some way. Something carries you all along. Do you think I don't know you are planning things and doing things?

Why cannot I—help you? I know this place, these people.
I am a sort of queen here. Am I nothing at all to
you?"

Cabal looks at her now intently. Is she trying to find out
about his plans of escape in order to betray him to the Boss?
Or is she proposing to betray the Boss to him? Or is she in a
state of mixed intrigue, ready to do either and mainly
interested in getting some love-making going?

He says: "And could you really restore me to my aeroplane? Hasn't that been put out of action?"

Roxana: "No. *He* wants to use it and doesn't know how to.
No one has touched it. There it is. With six guards night
and day. Even *I* could not get at that just now."

Cabal, who has been leaning against the table, stands up
and confronts her. She faces up to him.

Cabal: "What are you really proposing to me?"

Roxana: "Nothing. I came to see you. I was interested
in you."

Cabal: "Well?"

Roxana: "And now I find you more interesting than ever.
A woman loves to help. She loves to give. I could give so
much—*now*. And if I gave——?"

Cabal speaking like a representative: "The Air League
would not forget it."

Roxana: "The Air League will not forget! Air League!
Who cares for the Air League? Would *you* forget it?"

Cabal: "Why should I in particular——"

Roxana: "Are you stupid, man? Or are you insulting me?
I tell you I find you the most interesting man in the world,
a great eagle out of the air. And you stare at me with that
ugly face of yours and pretend not to understand! Have you
never met a woman before? Ugly you are and grey. It doesn't
matter."

Her manner changes. She comes close up to him and holds out her hands as if disposed to clutch his arms. "Oh why should I go on fencing with you? Don't you see—don't you understand? I'm for you—if you want me. I'm yours. You big strong thing, all steel and dignity. *Now*—now will you let me help you?"

They both become aware of a movement outside. She recoils quickly. The door is flung open without ceremony and the Boss appears in the doorway. He is wearing his conception of ceremonial uniform. In a rough way he has a certain splendour. He stands posed for a moment.

Boss: "So *this* is where you are!"

Roxana: "I said I should talk to him and I have."

Boss: "I told you to leave him alone."

Roxana: "Yes, and sat up there drinking and looking as wonderful and powerful as you could. Rudolf the Victorious! I know—you sent twice to ask Gordon and his wife to come! So that she should see you in your glory. And here am I trying to find out for you what this black invader *means*. Do you think I *wanted* to come and talk to him"—she turns to Cabal—"this grey cold man? While you are swaggering here, more aeroplanes are getting ready away there at Basra."

Boss: "Basra?"

Roxana: "His headquarters. Have you never heard of Basra?"

Boss: "These are matters for *men* to talk about."

Cabal: "Your lady has been putting me through a severe cross-examination. But the gist is—that away there in Basra the aeroplanes are rising night and day like hornets about a hornets' nest. What happens to me here, is a small affair. They'll *get* you. The new world of the united airmen will *get* you. Why, listen! You can almost hear them coming now."

The imagination of the Boss is caught for a moment and then it recovers. "Not a bit of it!"

Roxana: "What he says is the truth."

Boss: "What he says is *bluff*."

Roxana: "Make peace with the airmen and let him go."

Boss: "That means surrender of our sovereign independence."

Roxana: "But others will be coming. More machines and more."

Boss: "And he is here—hostage for their good behaviour. Come, my lady. An end to this little—*diplomatic* excursion of yours."

He holds the door open for her.

Roxana bridles. Is about to speak and goes out.

At the door she turns and fires a parting shot at the Boss.

"You have the subtlety of a——" She searches for a suitable epithet and then jumps at the word she needs. "Bullfrog."

When she has gone out of the room the Boss turns and comes towards Cabal.

Boss: "I don't know what she has been saying to you. Perhaps I don't care. Not as much as she thinks. There's no following her chopping and changing. I've had about enough of it. But I'm not a fool. There's no making peace between you and me. None at all. It's your world or mine. It's going to be mine—or I die fighting. After all this threatening—swarms of hornets and so on—you are a hostage. Understand. No one comes near you. Your friend Gordon will have to manage without you. And don't be so sure you'll win. So just go on sitting here and thinking about it, Mr. Wings over the World."

The following day, bright daylight, shining into the

laboratory of Dr. Harding. Mary leans against the work bench and Roxana is talking to her.

Roxana: "It is not only that I want to protect you from the insults of the Chief. Oh! I know him. But I want to talk to you about this man Cabal and this Airmen's world they talk about. What is this new world that is coming? Is it a *new* world really? Or only the old world dressed up in a new way? Do you understand Cabal? Is he flesh and blood?"

Mary: "He's a great man. My father knew him years ago. My husband worships him."

Roxana: "He's so cold—so preoccupied. And so—interesting. Do men like that ever make love?"

Mary: "A different sort of love, perhaps."

Roxana: "Love on ice. If this new world—all airships and science and order—comes about, what will happen to us women?"

Mary: "We shall work like the men."

Roxana: "You *mean* that? Are *you*—flesh and blood?"

Mary: "As much as my husband and father."

Roxana with infinite contempt: "*Men!* Sometimes—when I think of lean grim Cabal—I believe this world of yours *must* come. And then I think—it *can't* come. It can't. It's a dream. It will *seem* to come but it won't come. It's just a new lot of men at the top. There will be wars still. Struggles still."

Mary: "No, it will be civilisation. It will be peace. This nightmare of a world we live in—that is the dream, that is what will pass away."

Roxana: "No. No. *This* is reality."

Mary, staring in front of her: "Do you really think that war and struggle—mere chance gleams of happiness—general misery—all this squalid divided world about us, do you think it must go on for ever?"

Roxana: "You want an *impossible* world. Nice in a way—

perhaps—but impossible. You are asking too much from men and women. They won't *bother* to bring it about. You are asking them to want unnatural things. What do *we* want? We women. Knowledge, civilisation, the good of mankind? Nonsense! Oh, nonsense. We want satisfaction. We want glory. I want the glory of being loved—the glory of being wanted—desired, splendidly desired—and the glory of feeling and looking splendid. Do you want anything different? No. But you haven't learnt to look facts in the face yet. I know men. Every man wants the same thing—glory! Glory in some form. The glory of being loved—don't I know it? The glory they love most of all. The glory of bossing things here—the glory of war and victory. This brave new world of yours will never come. This wonderful world of reason! It wouldn't be worth having if it does come. It would be dull and safe and—oh, dreary! No lovers—no warriors—no dangers—no adventure."

Mary: "No adventure! No glory in helping to make the world over—anew! It is *you* who are dreaming."

Roxana: "Helping *men!* Why should we work and toil for men? Let them work and toil for us."

Mary: "But we can work *with* them!"

Roxana: "And what will *they* have to work for, then?"

Mary: "Greater things."

Roxana: "There's no flavour in those greater things. No flavour. No flavour at all. These airmen—they will conquer the world. And then we shall conquer *them*—lean and stern and sober though they are."

Mary: "If I thought that was all we could do——"

Roxana: "It *is* all we can do. Haven't you learnt anything from marriage with Gordon?"

Mary looks at her, detesting her. But she finds herself at a loss for an argument.

F

The noise of an aeroplane is heard growing rapidly louder. They turn to the window and look out. They become excited.

They crane up at an aeroplane circling overhead. It makes a great old-fashioned roar.

Roxana: "Look! It's your Gordon, he's flying at last."

The aeroplane, flying. In the aeroplane is Gordon at the controls. He is satisfied. Behind him sits a rosetted guard. Gordon turning the machine round. Then a long shot of Everytown far below. The machine flies on. The guard stirs. He protests inaudibly because of the roar of the engine. Gordon disregards him. Guard taps Gordon's shoulder, signs for him to return and presently, finding no response but a cheerful smile, points his pistol. Mutual scrutiny. Guard weakly menacing. Gordon points over the side of the cockpit. He smiles suddenly, having taken the measure of his man, and puts his fingers to his nose. The aeroplane jerks sharply upwards, and the guard, no longer pointing his pistol, but gripping tight, is manifestly scared.

Aeroplane looping the loop—then the falling leaf trick.

Guard's ordeal through all this motion. He drops the pistol and grips the side.

Pistol falling. Hitting the ground and exploding.

The aeroplane seen flying away over the hills.

"And so I got away," says Gordon's voice.

As the voice is heard, the last scene dissolves into the next.

A conference room at Basra, rather like an ultra-modern board room. It is bleakly and rationally furnished. Telephones have been restored to the world. Through a large open window one sees the great and growing aerodrome of Basra with a number of aeroplanes coming and going. Far off there is a group of smoking factory chimneys. It is a sudden contrast to the general ruinousness that has prevailed throughout this film since the war sequences. A dozen young and middle-aged men sit at the table indifferent to these familiar activities outside, and Gordon stands talking—too excited to sit.

Gordon: "And so I got away. That is where you will find Cabal. The Boss of Everytown is a violent Tough—he may do anything. There is no time to lose."

A Middle-aged Man: "Certainly, there is no time to lose. Half squadron A is ready now. You ready to go with them, Mr.——?"

Gordon : "Gordon, sir."

The middle-aged man begins to dial a telephone.

A Young Man: "This gives us a chance of trying this new anæsthetic, the Gas of Peace . . . I wish *I* could go . . ."

Wipe off to next scene.

The Boss's bedroom. It is a large untidy room furnished with the best loot of the district. The Boss is in *déshabillé*, and has just got out of bed. He is still heavy with sleep. With him is Burton and by the door stands a messenger.

Burton: "At last we have definite news."

Boss: "What is it?"

An attendant brings in a tray of breakfast, and sets it on the table.

Burton: "Gordon didn't fall into the sea. He got away. A fishing boat saw him making the French coast. Perhaps he reached his pals."

Boss, disagreeably: "Well?"

Burton: "He'll be coming back. He'll be bringing the others with him."

Attendant leaves.

The Boss is waking up slowly and is very peevish: "Curse this Air League. Curse all airmen and gas men and machine men! Why didn't we leave their machines and chemicals alone. I might have known. Why did I tamper with flying?"

Burton: "Well, we needed aeroplanes—against the Hill State. Somebody else would have started in again with aeroplanes and gas and bombs if we hadn't. These people would have come interfering anyhow."

Boss: "Why was all this science ever allowed? Why was it ever let begin?" He turns listlessly to his breakfast. He begins again: "Science!—it's the enemy of everything that is natural in life. I dreamt of those chaps in the night. Great ugly inhuman chaps in black. Half like machines. Bombing and bombing."

Burton: "I guess they'll come bombing, all right."

Boss: "Then we'll fight 'em. Since Gordon got away I've had one or two of the air boys to see me. Those boys have guts. They can do something still."

He walks up and down devouring a piece of bread. "We'll fight 'em. We'll fight 'em. We've got hostages. . . . I'm glad now we haven't shot *them* anyhow. `I wonder if that fellow Harding. . . . Of course! He can tell us what to do about this gas. If we have to wring his arm off and knock half his teeth down his throat to make him do it. Get him—*get* him."

Burton at door shouting for men and giving orders

The Boss is gathering courage and takes his food with greater gusto: "They have to come to earth sometime. What is this World Communications? A handful of men like ourselves. They're not *magic*."

A row of old and worn-out aeroplanes in front of a battered hangar. A number of very young inexperienced-looking pilots stand before them. The Boss is inspecting them. Roxana is beside him.

The Boss begins his speech: "To you I entrust these good, these tried and tested machines. You are not mechanics—

you are warriors. You have been taught not to think, but to do—and—if need be, die. I salute you—I, your leader."

The boy pilots go off rather reluctantly to their machines and start them up. It is an almost " Heath Robinson " scene of our contemporary (1935) machines in the last stage of decay and patch-up.

A very long shot of a new type of air bomber flying with a sort of remorselessness—in contrast with the hops and misbehaviour of the Boss's machines. It is Gordon returning. Two other big bombers follow, low down in the sky.

This machine has a distinctive throb of its own which should mingle with the menace of the music.

Closer shots of parts of this great bomber. Aviators (three men and two women) stand about looking down on the world. One is Gordon. Gordon is anxious.

A large cavernous space arched over by the girder of a fallen building. It looks out upon suburban ruins and a distant hillside. The Boss is with Burton and Roxana and his staff. The Boss studies the familiar skyline through binoculars. Guards bring in Mary and Harding. The Boss turns to them.

Boss: "What do you know about these Air League people? Have they gas? What sort of gas?"

Harding: "I know nothing of gas."

Boss: "Here, where are the masks?"

Two boys appear with a job lot of masks—caricatures of existing types.

Boss: "Tell us about these masks, anyhow."

Harding examines a mask and tears it and throws it down. "Rotten! No use at all."

Boss: "What gas have they got?"

Harding: "Gas war isn't my business."

Boss: "Well, they can't gas us when *you* are here anyhow."

Burton, in dismay: "Here they are. Listen. They're coming already!"

The strange recognisable throb of Gordon's aeroplanes is heard and the music that accompanies it, gradually getting louder.

The Boss rushes forward and looks up with his binoculars: "Clumsy great things! Our boys will have them down in five minutes. They're too clumsy. What!—only six of us up. Where are the rest of our fellows?"

Sudden consternation of the group at something unseen. A machine falls in flames and crashes in the distance.

Boss: "Go on—*up* at him."

A loud report. Far off another aeroplane crashes in flames.

Roxana: "Poor boy—it's got him."

Boss: "They're both coming down. Cowards!"

Roxana: "But they can't use gas—how *can* they use gas?—when we have the hostages."

The Boss turns and looks at the hostages. "Ah! the hostages! I'm not done yet. Lead them out—there. Tie 'em up. Out there in the open. Where they can be seen."

Guards take Mary and Harding out to the open and tie them up to two posts. Closer shot of Mary and Harding being tied to the posts. They look at one another with steady eyes. Then they look up at the sky.

The Boss comes over to them, brandishing his pistol. He shouts up to the sky: "Come down, or I shoot them. Are you bombing your own hostages? Come down or I shoot."

He remembers Cabal. "Where's the other fellow? He's the

Prize Hostage. He's the best of all. They'll know him. Four of you—go and fetch him. . . ."

A deep soft thud and a bomb explodes some distance off. The sound the bomb makes is not a sharp explosive report; it is more like the whoof of a puff of steam.

A Soldier cries out: "Is it gas?"

The Boss waves his pistol at Mary and Harding. "You anyhow, shall die before I do." Roxana stands near him. Another bomb thuds nearer. The Boss points his pistol at Harding with an expression of desperate resolution, but Roxana knocks it up as he fires.

Boss : "*You* turn against me?"

Roxana: "Don't you see—he's beaten you. Look!"

Soldiers in the distance are seen staggering and falling.

The gas this time is transparent, and is available only as a sort of shimmering heat haze. The foreground now is still perfectly clear, but the middle distance is *flickering*.

Roxana rushes to Mary and clings to her: "Mary—I never did you any harm. I saved your father. I saved you. Couldn't you call up to your man—to stop this . . ."

Crescendo of whoofs close at hand. Whoof. *Whoof.* WHOOF. The gas increases and creeps nearer and nearer. The picture concentrates on the face of the Boss.

The Boss looks with amazement at his men gradually succumbing to the gas. He starts and pulls himself together.

Boss: "Shoot them—what are you all doing—why don't you move. I won't have it like this. What's happening? Everything is going swimmy! Everything is swimming."

He wipes his hand across his eyes as if he can no longer see or think distinctly. He wipes his mouth and rubs his eyes. His face is suddenly distorted in a last violent effort to resist the gas.

The flicker of the gas is now all over the screen. The

flickering becomes violent so that it is as if one saw the face of the Boss through disturbed water.

Boss: "Shoot, I say! Shoot. Shoot. We've never shot enough yet. We never shot enough. We spared them. These intellectuals! These contrivers! These experts! Now they've *got us*. Our world or theirs. What did a few hundreds of them matter? We've been weak—*weak*. Kill them like vermin! Kill all of them! . . . Why should I be beaten like this? Weakness! Weakness! Weakness is fatal. . . . Shoot!"

The flickering broadens out to a swirling dissolve of outwardly moving circles.

The dark figure of Cabal appears through the swirl. He is wearing his great mask again and there is no sign of collapse about him.

Cabal: "Your sentries seem to have gone to sleep. So I came out. . . . All the town is going to sleep. . . . You made us do it."

Abruptly the picture becomes clear again. The Boss sprawls headlong as it does so. As he becomes insensible you are no longer supposed to see things with his eyes. He falls exactly at the moment when the swirling ends. The tall black figure of Cabal now stands up in the foreground.

All the rest are lying insensible before him. . . .

Pause.

Cabal: "And now for the World of the Airmen and a new start for mankind."

The camera pauses at the side of Cabal so that only the side of his head and shoulders and arm frame the picture. You do not get Cabal all in the picture again. You see the profile of his mask and his black arm and hand.

Mary is in a sitting position at the foot of the post to which she was tied and Roxana is grouped very gracefully across her feet. The Boss sprawls on his face in the foreground with his clenched fist outstretched. Harding droops from his post. Burton a little further off lies on a heap of rubble and beyond are soldiers and attendants. Cabal comes nearer to the group. "You might be more comfortable, Harding," he says, and releases the ropes, lowering the inanimate Harding into a sitting position. "So."

Then he turns to the two women. "Well, my dears, you must sleep for a time. There's nothing more to be done."

He stands looking at them. Close up of the two women's faces in repose. Mary is quietly peaceful. Roxana even when she is insensible contrives to be attractive. Cabal's voice is heard.

Cabal: "Mary. And Madame Roxana! Queer contrast. Madame Roxana. A pretty thing and a very pretty thing and what's to be done with this very pretty thing? The eternal adventuress. A common pretty woman who doesn't work. A lady! She has pluck. Charm. Brains enought for infinite mischief. And a sort of energy. She'll play her pretty eyes at men to the end of her time. Now the Bosses go the way of the money grubbers, I suppose it will be our turn. Wherever power is, she will follow. And let me confess to you, young woman, now that you can't hear me or take any advantage of me, that considering my high responsibilities and my dignified years, I find you a lot more interesting and disturbing than I ought to do. Men are men, you said, to the end of their days. You *get* at us. I wish we could keep you under gas always. There is much to be said for the harem idea. Must you still be up to your tricks in our new world?"

The view of the camera widens to take in all the slumbering bodies.

Cabal: "The new world, with the old stuff. Our job is only beginning."

Dawn breaking over Everytown. Dawn sky. Vista of a side

street. Sleeping figures lie scattered about. Gordon and a knot of companions, several young airmen and two women, also in black leather, come through the ruins. They are no longer masked. One of them tears down a rosette flag in passing.

First Young Airman: "They'll sleep for another day."

Second Airman: "Well, we've given 'em a whiff of civilisation at last."

First Airman: "Nothing like putting children to sleep when they are naughty."

On the outskirts of the town, wondering country people in their coarse canvas clothes and sabots are seen coming down the hillside against the familiar skyline.

People coming into the Square which is littered with sleepers. Some of the sleepers are beginning to stir. A bunch of the new airmen in their black costumes, but not masked or helmeted, appear and walk across the scene.

People staring at the airmen, the backs of the unkempt heads very big in silhouette in the foreground of the picture.

It is decadent barbarism watching the return of civilisation.

Return to the council room, the board room, at the aerodrome at Basra. Much greater activity is now seen through the window. Big lorries are running about. People go to and fro. Aeroplanes of novel type are going up in groups of seven, squadron after squadron.

The table is now covered with maps and a group of secretaries stand ready to give any help. Costumes, very slightly "futuristic," severe, and mostly mechanics' or air costume.

The same council is present, but in addition Cabal is now a dominant figure beside the Chairman.

Cabal, leaning over a map: "This is how I conceive our plan of operations. Settle, organise, advance. This zone, then that. At last wings over the whole world and the new world begins. More and more it will become a round-up of brigands. . . ."

The Airmen's War. Many aeroplanes of strange and novel shape rising into the air. They fill the sky. A brief air fight between three old normal fighting aeroplanes and one of the new aeroplanes.

Over a ruinous landscape, brigands with flags and old military uniforms in flight as the new aeroplanes overhead bomb them. The bombs explode and gas overcomes the brigands.

Sky writing by the new planes: SURRENDER.

Brigands crawl from hiding places and surrender, hands over their heads. Brigands run out from the houses of another town as the aeroplanes approach. They surrender.

The sky dotted with the new aeroplanes. Hundreds of men drop from the sky with parachutes. The brigands stand waiting.

A line of prisoners marching. They carry regimental flags. They are the last ragged vestige of the regular armies of the old order. It is the end of organised war at last. A group of the new airmen watch their march-past. Overhead the new aeroplanes are hovering.

PART X

Reconstruction

THE object of this Part is to bridge, as rapidly and vigorously as possible, the transition from the year 1970 to the year 2054. An age of enormous mechanical and industrial energy has to be suggested by a few moments of picture and music. The music should begin with a monstrous clangour and come down to a smoother and smoother rhythm as efficiency prevails over stress. The shots dissolve rapidly on to one another, and are bridged with enigmatic and eccentric mechanical movements. The small figures of men move among the monstrosities of mechanism, more and more dwarfed by their accumulating intensity.

An explosive blast fills the screen. The smoke clears, and the work of the engineers of this new age looms upon us. First, there is a great clearance of old material and a preparation for new structures. Gigantic cranes swing across the screen. Old ruined steel frameworks are torn down. Shots are given of the clearing up of old buildings and ruins.

Then come shots suggesting experiment, design and the making of new materials. A huge power station and machine details are shown. Digging machines are seen making a gigantic excavation. Conveyer belts carry away the debris. Stress is laid on the work of excavation because the Everytown of the year 2054 will be dug into the hills. It will not be a skyscraper city.

A chemical factory with a dark liquid bubbling in giant retorts, works swiftly and smoothly. Masked workers go to and fro. The liquid is poured out into a moulding machine that is making walls for new buildings.

The metal scaffolding of the new town is being made and great slabs of wall from the moulding machine are placed in position. The lines of the new subterranean city of Everytown begin to appear, bold and colossal.

Swirling river rapids are seen giving place to a deep controlled flow of water as a symbol of material civilisation gaining control of nature.

A fantasia of powerful rotating and swinging forms carried on a broad stream of music concludes this Part.

Flash the date A.D. 2054.

A loud querulous voice breaks across the concluding phase of this "Transition" music. "I don't *like* these mechanical triumphs."

The voice is the voice of Theotocopulos, the rebel artist of the new era. His face becomes visible, very big on the screen. He speaks with force and bitterness: "I do not like this machinery. I do not *like* this machinery. All these wheels going round. Everything going so fast and slick. *No*."

The camera recedes from him until he is seen to be sitting at the foot of a great mass of marble. He is wearing the white overalls of a sculptor and carries a mallet and a chisel.

A second sculptor, a bearded man, comes into the picture. "Well, what can we do about it?"

Theotocopulos, as if he reveals the most obscure secret, "*Talk*."

The bearded man shrugs his shoulders and grimaces humorously as if towards a third interlocutor in the auditorium.

Theotocopulos explodes: "Talk. Radio is everywhere. *This modern world is full of voices. I* am going to talk all this machinery down."

The Bearded Man: "But will they let you ?"

Theotocopulos imperiously: "They'll let me. I shall call my talks, *Art and Life*. That sounds harmless enough. And I will *go* for this Brave New World of theirs—tooth and claw."

Flash back to date.

A.D. 2054.

PART XI

The Little Girl Learns about the New World

A LARGE space, rather than a room, partaking of the nature of a conservatory and large drawing-room. There are neither pillars nor right-angle joins. The roof curves gently over the space. Beautiful plants and a fountain in a basin. Through the plants one catches a glimpse of the City Ways. An old gentleman of a hundred and ten years or thereabouts, but good-looking and well-preserved, sits in an arm-chair. A pretty little girl (8-9) lies on a couch and looks at a piece of apparatus on which pictures appear. It has a simple control knob. Some strange pet animal, perhaps a capuchin monkey, is playing with a ball on the rug. A doll in an exaggerated costume of the period lies on a seat.

Girl: "I like these History Lessons."

The apparatus is showing Lower New York from above —an aeroplane travelogue.

Little Girl: "What a funny place New York was—all sticking up and full of windows."

Old Man: "They built houses like that in the old days."

Little Girl: "Why?"

Old Man: "They had no light inside their cities as we have. So they had to stick the houses up into the daylight— what there was of it. They had no properly mixed and conditioned air."

He manipulates the knob and shows a similar view of Paris or Berlin. "Everybody lived half out of doors. And windows of soft brittle glass everywhere. The Age of Windows lasted four centuries."

The apparatus shows rows of windows, cracked, broken,

mended, étc. It is a brief fantasia on the theme of windows done in the Grierson style.

Old Man: "They never seemed to realise that we could light the interiors of our houses with sunshine of our own, so that there would be no need to poke our houses up ever so high into the air."

Little Girl: "Weren't the people *tired* going up and down those stairs?"

Old Man: "They were *all* tired and they had a disease called colds. Everybody had colds and coughed and sneezed and ran at the eyes."

Little Girl: "What's *sneezed?*"

Old Man: "*You* know. Atishoo!"

The little girl sits up very greatly delighted.

Little Girl: "Atishoo. Everyone said Atishoo. That *must* have been funny."

Old Man: "Not so funny as you think."

Little Girl: "And you remember all that, great-grand-father?"

Old Man: "I remember some of it. Colds we had and we had indigestion too—from the queer bad foods we ate. It was a poor life. Never really *well*."

Little Girl: "Did people laugh at it?"

Old Man: "They *had* a way of grinning at it. They called it humour. We had to have a lot of humour. I've lived through some horrid times, my dear. Oh! Horrid!"

Little Girl: "Horrid! I don't want to see or hear about that. The Wars, the Wandering Sickness and all those dreadful years. None of that will come again, great-grand-dad? Ever?"

Old Man: "Not if progress goes on."

Little Girl: "They keep on inventing new things now, don't they? And making life lovelier and lovelier?"

Old Man: "Yes. . . . Lovelier—and bolder. . . . I suppose I'm an old man, my dear, but some of it seems almost like going too far. This Space Gun of theirs that they keep on shooting."

Little Girl: "What *is* this Space Gun, great-grandfather?"

Old Man: "It is a gun they discharge by electricity—it's a lot of guns one inside the other—each one discharges the next inside. I don't properly understand that. But the cylinder it shoots out at last, goes so fast that it goes—swish—right away from the earth."

Little Girl (entranced): "What! Right out into the sky! To the stars?"

Old Man: "They may get to the stars in time, but what they shoot at now is the moon."

Little Girl: "You mean they shoot cylinders at the moon! Poor old moon!"

Old Man: "Not exactly *at* it. They shoot the cylinder so that it travels round the other side of the moon and comes back and there's a safe place in the Pacific Ocean where it drops. They get more and more accurate. They say they can tell within twenty miles where it will come back and they keep the sea clear for it. You see?"

Little Girl: "But how splendid. And can people go in the cylinders? Can I go when I grow up? And see the other side of the moon ! And plump back *ker-splosh*! into the sea!"

Old Man: "Oh! They haven't sent men and women yet. that's what all the trouble's about. That's what Theoto-copulos is making the trouble about."

Little Girl: "Theo—cotto——"

Old Man: "Theotocopulos."

Little Girl: "What a funny name!"

Old Man: "It's a Greek name. He's the descendant of a great artist called El Greco. *Theótocopulos*—like that."

Little Girl: "And he makes trouble you say?"

Old Man: "Oh, never mind."

Little Girl: "It wouldn't *hurt* to go to the moon?"

Old Man: "We don't know. Some people say yes—some people say no. They've sent mice round."

Little Girl: "Mice that have gone round the moon!"

Old Man: "They get broken up, poor little beasties! They don't know how to hold on when the bumps come. That's why there's all this talk of sending a man, perhaps. He'd know how to hold on. . . ."

Little Girl: "He'd have to be brave, wouldn't he? . . . I wish I could fly round the moon."

Old Man: "That in time, my dear. Won't you come back to your history pictures again?"

Little Girl : "I'm glad I didn't live in the old world. I know that John Cabal and his airmen tidied it up. Did you *see* John Cabal, great-grand-dad?"

Old Man: "You can see him in your pictures, my dear."

Little Girl: "But you saw him when he lived, you really *saw* him?"

Old Man: "Yes. I saw the great John Cabal with my own eyes when I was a little boy. A lean brown old man with hair as white as mine."

A still of John Cabal is shown as we saw him in the council at Basra.

The Old Man adds: "He was the grandfather of *our* Oswald Cabal, the President of our Council."

Little Girl: "Just as you are my *great*-grandfather?"

The old man pats the little girl.

The scene should be wiped out by the next presentation, which shows a hand and an arm on a table. The arm carries a light gauntlet and on the gauntlet is a kind of identification disk on which one reads the words: "Oswald Cabal, President of the Council of Direction."

Such identification plates on the wrists or arms are a usual feature of the costume of the period.

PART XII

The New Generation

THIS hand and arm is held for a moment. The fingers drum on the table in a manner reminiscent of John Cabal in Part I. It is an inherited habit. Then the camera recedes to show Oswald Cabal seated in his private room in the administrative offices of the city of Everytown.

The room is of the same easy style of architecture as the preceding scene. There are no windows and no corners, but across a kind of animated frieze, a band of wall, above Cabal's head, there sweep phantom clouds and waves, waving trees, clusters of flowers and the like in a perpetual silent sequence of decorative effects. There is a large televisor disk and telephone and other apparatus on the desk before Cabal.

Oswald Cabal is a calmer, younger-looking version of his ancestor. His hair is dark and like all hair in the new world trimly dressed. His costume is of a white silken material with very slight and simple embroidery. In its fineness and whiteness and in its breadth across the shoulders it contrasts acutely with the close black aviator costume of John Cabal.

Cabal says to an unseen interlocutor : "Then I take it this Space Gun has passed all its preliminary trials and that nothing remains now but the selection of those who are to go."

The picture broadens out, and we see that Cabal is not alone. He is in conference with two engineers. They wear dark and simple clothes in the broad-shouldered fashion of the age—not leather working-clothes or anything of that sort. In an age of mechanical perfection there is no need for overalls and grease-proof clothing. One sits on a chair of modernist form. (All furniture is metallic.) The other leans familiarly against a table.

First Engineer: "That's going to be the trouble."

Second Engineer: "There are thousands of young people applying—young men and young women. I never dreamt the moon was so attractive."

First Engineer: "Practically the gun is perfect now. There are risks but reasonable risks. And the position of the moon in the next three or four months gives us the best conditions for getting there. It is only the choice of the two now that matters."

Cabal: "Well?"

Second Engineer: "There are going to be difficulties. That man Theotocopulos is talking on the radio about it."

Cabal: "He's a fantastic creature."

Second Engineer: "Yes, but he is making trouble. It is not going to be easy to choose these young people."

Cabal: "With all those thousands offering?"

First Engineer: "We have looked into thousands of cases. We have rejected everyone of imperfect health. Or anyone who had friends who objected. And the fact is, Sir——. We wish you would talk to two people. There is Raymond Passworthy of General Fabrics. You know him?"

Cabal: "Quite well. His great-grandfather knew mine."

First Engineer: "And his son."

Second Engineer: "We want you to see the son, Sir—Maurice Passworthy."

Cabal: "Why?"

First Engineer: "He asks to go."

Cabal: "With whom?"

Second Engineer : "We think you had better see him. He is waiting here."

Cabal considers and then lifts his gauntlet and touches a spot on it. A faint musical sound responds. He says : "Is Maurice Passworthy waiting. . . . Yes. . . . Send him up."

Almost immediately a panel opens in the wall and a slender, rather lightly-clad, good-looking young man appears.

Cabal stands up and looks at him. "You want to talk with me?"

The two engineers bow and retire.

Maurice Passworthy: "Forgive me, Sir. I came straight to you."

Cabal: "You ask a favour?"

Maurice Passworthy: "A very big favour. I want to be one of the first two human beings to see the other side of the moon."

Cabal: "It means danger. Great hardship anyhow. There is an even chance, they say, you may never come back. And a still greater chance of coming back crippled."

Maurice Passworthy: "Give me credit for not minding that, Sir."

Cabal: "A lot of you young people don't mind that. But why should *you* be favoured?"

Maurice Passworthy: "Well, Sir, I'm the son of a friend of yours. People seem to feel—you ought not to send two people you do not know——" He leaves his sentence unfinished.

Cabal: "Go on."

Maurice Passworthy: "We have talked about this over and over again."

Cabal: "*We?*"

Maurice Passworthy: "You stand for so much in the New World, the Great World of to-day."

Cabal is leaning against his desk and thinking. He looks keenly at the young man's face. "*We?*" he repeats.

Maurice Passworthy: "Both of us. It is her idea even more than it is mine."

Cabal's mind has already leapt forward to what is coming. "*Her* idea? Who is she?"

Maurice Passworthy: "Some one much closer to you than I am, Sir."

Cabal, quietly: "Tell me."

Maurice Passworthy: "We have been fellow students these three years."

Cabal impatiently: "Yes—yes but tell me."

Maurice Passworthy: "It is your daughter, Sir—Catherine. She says that you cannot possibly send anyone's child but your own."

Cabal after a pause: "I might have known."

Maurice Passworthy: "You see, Sir——"

Cabal: "I see. My daughter. . . . Funny that I never thought of her as anything but a little girl. Quite out of this. . . . My Catherine."

Maurice Passworthy: "She is eighteen."

Cabal: "A *ripe* age. . . . I'm a little—taken by surprise. And you two have thought it all out."

Maurice Passworthy: "It's so plain, Sir."

Cabal: "Yes, it's plain. It's just. It is exactly as things ought to be. Exactly. All these other thousands will have to wait their turn. . . . Sit down here. Tell me how first you came to know my Catherine?"

Maurice Passworthy: "Ever since we began to work together. It seemed so natural, Sir. She's so straight and simple. . . ."

Cabal and Maurice Passworthy sit down for a talk and the pictures fades out. Cabal has still to assimilate this novel idea.

Close up of Cabal. It is half an hour later. He is no longer in his bureau. He is standing in a dark recess against a gracefully patterned wall. A small clear sound is heard and he attends to the telephone disk on his gauntlet. "Yes. . . . Who is it? . . . Raymond Passworthy. . . . Certainly. . . ."

He waits for half a second. "Is that Raymond Passworthy? Yes. I have been talking to your son for half an hour. Yes. He is a splendid youngster. . . . You want to talk to me. At your service. . . . I am going to see my daughter at the Athletic Club. He is meeting her there. He has just gone to her. Would you care to walk with me through the City Ways and out through the weather? . . . I'll be with you. . . ."

Scene changes to a view of one of the high-flung City Ways in the brightly-lit cavernous Everytown of 2055.

Here for the first time one sees the ordinary social types of the year 2055 at close hand, their costume and their bearing. No one is ragged and only one man is wearing any sort of working costume. He is a gardener and he is spraying some of the flowers. The general type of costume is reminiscent of men's costume in Tudor days, varying very widely between simplicity and ornateness (see Memorandum *ante*). Some of the young women are very lightly and simply clad, but others are more consciously "costumed." One sees also the very bold and decorative architecture of this semi-sub-terranean city and the use of running water and novel and beautiful plants and flowering shrubs in decoration. In the sustained bright light and conditioned air of the new Every-town, and in the hands of skilful gardeners, vegetation has taken on a new vigour and loveliness. People pass. People gather in knots and look down on the great spaces below.

The figures of Cabal and Passworthy come walking across the foreground of this scene. Passworthy is a finer, fitter version, leaner, cleaner and trimmer, of his ancestor the Passworthy of the opening scenes. He walks talking with Cabal for some paces, with the city scene passing panorama fashion behind, and then the two come to a stop, leaning against a parapet looking down on the city and talking earnestly.

Passworthy: "I grant you the reality of the progress the world has made since the Airmen took control. It has been a century of marvels. But cannot we have too much of pro-gress? Here I agree is a lovely world in which we are living. A little artificial—but admirable at last. The triumph of human invention and human will. Comfort, beauty, security. Our light is brighter than the sunshine outside and never before has mankind breathed so sweet an air. We have got the better of nature. Why should we still drive on so urgently?"

Cabal: "Because it is in the nature of life to drive on. The most unnatural thing in life is contentment."

Passworthy: "Contentment! Contentment is Heaven!"

Cabal: "And this is not heaven."

Passworthy: "No. Indeed not. When sons rebel against their fathers."

Cabal: "And fathers listen to their daughters. We are both fathers of rebel children, eh? An old problem, Passworthy. A child that isn't a rebel is a vain repetition. What to do with our sons and daughters? Fathers like you and me were asking that question in the Stone Age."

Passworthy: "But to hurl them at the moon!"

Cabal: "They hurl themselves."

Passworthy: "Desperate young people. Why should they be willing?"

Cabal: "Humanity is tough stuff. If it wasn't for the desperate young people it wouldn't have got very far."

Passworthy: "Anyone who attempts such an expedition must be killed. You *know* that. Lost for ever on that frozen world."

Cabal: "They're not going *to* the moon; they're going round it."

Passworthy: "That's a quibble."

Cabal: "They will come back."

Passworthy: "If I could believe that!"

Cabal: "The best thing for us both is to believe it."

Passworthy: "Why should *our* children be chosen for a thing like this?"

Cabal: "Science asks for the best."

Passworthy: "But my boy! Always such an impetuous little devil. All very well for you, Cabal. You are the great-grandson of John Cabal, the air dictator—who changed the course of the world. Experiment is in your blood. You—and your daughter! I'm—I'm more *normal*. I don't believe my boy would ever have thought of it. But the two of them got together. They want to go together."

Cabal: "They will come back together. This time there is to be no attempt to land on the moon."

Passworthy: "And when is this—this great experiment to be made? How long are we to have them before they go?"

Cabal (a little disingenuously): "I don't know."

Passworthy: "But when?"

Cabal: "When the Space Gun is ready again."

Passworthy: "You mean some time this year?"

Cabal: "Soon."

Passworthy: "In the old days it was different. Fathers had authority then. I should have said 'No,' and that would have settled it."

Cabal: "Fathers have said 'No' since the Stone Age."

Passworthy: "And is there no saving of our children from this madness?"

Cabal: "But would it be saving our children?"

Passworthy: "Yes—it would."

Cabal: "For what?"

Passworthy (bursts out): "Children are born to be happy. Young people should take life lightly. There is something horrible in this immolation—it is nothing less than immolation—at eighteen and twenty-one."

Cabal: "Do you think I have no feelings like yours? That I don't love my daughter? . . . I'm snatching an hour to-day —just to see her and look at her while I can. All the same, I shall let her go . . . when the time comes."

Passworthy: "Where are they now?"

Cabal: "She is away at the Athletic Club in the hills—in training. Your son is there now. Come with me and see them. Face to face with them we may not feel just as we do here. Anyhow it will be well to be with them a bit. . . . It's fine outside. Will you come—do you mind coming out in the weather with me?"

Passworthy: "Mind? I'm an open-air man. This conditioned air may be better for us with its extra oxygen and so on, and the light here steadier and brighter, but give me the old sky and the wind on the heath, brother, and the

snow and the rain, the quick changes and the nightfall. I
don't really *love* this human ant-hill in which we live."

Cabal: "We'll go and talk to the young people."

The next scene is introduced chiefly to give an exterior
view of the new Everytown. The old familiar hill-contour
is in the background and quite recognisable, but the old
town itself under the open sky has disappeared and given
place to a few terraces and exterior structures. There are
unfamiliar architectural forms, grass slopes and formal trees.
It is very tranquil and beautiful, the apotheosis of Everytown. A few aeroplanes of novel structure pass across the sky.
Cabal and Passworthy have changed their costumes to
something more suitable for the open air, a fabric of the
cloth type instead of silky wear, and they have cloaks. The
sky is cloudy, the weather is showery, and in contrast to the
serenity of the city the sunlight drifts in patches across the
scene. Along a wide highway flows an almost noiseless
traffic of streamlined vehicles that come and go through a
great entrance, far more brightly lit than the world outside.

Passworthy (with an effort to be easy-minded): "Here we
are up in the weather. Back to Nature. Well, well—don't
you feel the better for it?"

Cabal: "If I did I should make trouble for our ventilation
department. I'll confess I like the varying breeze and the
shadows of the clouds—now and then."

Passworthy: "What changes those old hills there have seen
in the last two centuries. Prosperity. War. Want. Pestilence.
This New Amazing World. Look at it now."

Cabal: "And the changes they have seen are nothing to
the changes they are destined to see."

Passworthy: "Those old hills there. They are the only

things our great-grandfathers would recognise. I suppose they too in their turn will be swept away."

Cabal: "All things are swept away in their turn. Blame Nature for that, not man."

Passworthy: "There's some open-air people playing that old game of golf away there. It's a good game. I swing a club a bit myself. I don't suppose you do?"

Cabal: "I don't. Why should I?"

Passworthy: "It keeps one from thinking."

Cabal lifts his eyebrows.

Passworthy: "It couldn't keep me from thinking to-day anyhow. Oh! I can't keep my mind off it! These young people of ours! My heart aches. I feel it *here*. . . . I'm out of sorts with this modern world and all this progress. I suppose our city is all very fine and vital, and the countryside trimmer and lovelier—if you like—than it was in the days of competition and scramble. I suppose there is hardly a bramble or a swamp or a thicket left in the world. Why can't we rest at this? Why must we go on—and go on more strenuously than ever?"

Cabal: "Would you stop all thinking and working for ever more?"

Passworthy: "Oh, not exactly *that*."

Cabal: "Then what do you mean? A little thinking, but not very much? A little work but nothing serious?"

Passworthy: "Well, *Moderation*. Go on if you like—but go *easily*."

Cabal: "You think I drive? That my sort drives?"

Passworthy: "If you must have the truth—yes—you drive —*damnably*."

Cabal: "No. Nature drives. She drives and kills. She is man's mother, and she is his incessant enemy. She bears all her children in hate and struggle. Beneath this surface of plenty and security she is still contriving mischief. A hundred years ago she did her best with what she found in us, to keep our hands and hearts turned against each other and make us destroy ourselves by war. She added her own peculiar little contribution to that—the pestilence. Well, we won that battle. People forget already how hardly it was won. Now she wants to turn our very success against us, tempt us to be indolent, fantastic, idlers and pleasure-lovers—betraying ourselves in another fashion. A hundred years ago men like you said that war didn't matter, and it was my sort had to end it. And now you say going on doesn't matter. Life couldn't be better. Let the new generation *play*—waste the life that is in them. . . . A planet-load of holiday makers, spinning to destruction. Just a crowning festival before the dark."

The Hall of the Athletic Club. It is a glazed loggia, a half out-of-doors place, and it has immense windows of flexible glass. Outside are water chutes down which athletes (of either sex) flash with great swiftness. What they do is not very clear. It is as if they skied down a waterfall. You get only a dim impression of people flashing by and of rushing water and a rocky waterfall. A few spectators stand within the loggia, and there is a coming and going of young athletes and visitors. Cabal and Passworthy enter. They approach one of the immense windows. A spectator stands there already. The spectator follows excitedly the feats outside. He leans against the glass. The flexible glass gives to the pressure and produces a distorted view of the rocky scene outside. Then as the spectator withdraws his hand the window adjusts itself.

Passworthy: "Here again every day someone is injured or killed! Why should anyone be killed?"

Cabal: "Everything is done to eliminate the clumsy ones before an accident occurs. But how are we to save the race from degeneration unless this sort of thing goes on?"

Passworthy: "My God! Look at that fellow——"

Several spectators rush to the windows.

Cabal: "He's all right."

Passworthy: "And here they are!"

He directs Cabal's attention towards the doorway. From the doorway Catherine Cabal and Maurice Passworthy approach Cabal and Passworthy.

The two young people are now both in athletic costumes, very light, revealing their graceful young bodies. Catherine Cabal is a little slighter than Maurice, pretty but determined. They come forward to greet their parents, a little shyly. Maurice halts. Catherine goes up to her father, looks him in the eyes for a moment, is satisfied by what she sees there, and kisses him. He holds her to him for a moment and then releases her. Neither says a word.

Passworthy (trying to take things lightly): "Well, young people. What have you been doing?"

Maurice: "Just a turn at the water chutes. No time for anything else."

Passworthy: "How many killed to-day?"

Maurice: "No one. One fellow slipped and broke his thigh —but he's being taken care of. He'll be well in a week. I just missed him as he fell. Or I might have come a cropper too."

Passworthy: "Isn't life dangerous enough without doing these things?"

Maurice: "My dear Father, it isn't nearly dangerous enough for a properly constituted animal. Since the world began life has been living by the skin of its teeth. It's used to it and it's built that way. And that's what's the matter with us now."

Passworthy: "That's *your* philosophy, Cabal. My boy has learnt his lesson."

Cabal: "Not *my* philosophy. The philosophy of the new world."

Pause.

Catherine, unable to remain uncertain any longer: "Father, are we to go?"

Cabal: "Yes—you are to go."

Catherine: "It is announced?"

Cabal: "Yes."

Passworthy, dismayed: "It's announced?"

Cabal: "Why not?"

Passworthy: "But—my *son!*"

Cabal: "The boy is of age. He has volunteered."

Passworthy: "But I want to talk it over first. I want to talk it over. Why have you announced it so soon? Anyhow there is still plenty of time to talk it over."

A pause. Very intense scrutiny of faces. Catherine and Maurice look at each other and then at their parents.

Maurice: "Not so very long now, Father."

Catherine seems about to speak but does not do so.

Passworthy: "I suppose we have some *months* yet."

Catherine: "It is just one month and three days. Everything is ready *now*."

Maurice: "We could go now. The moon is coming into the right position even while we are talking. But they are waiting a month longer. To make sure."

Passworthy: "You are going in four weeks! Four weeks! I forbid it!"

Cabal: "I thought——"

Maurice: "No, it's all arranged."

Passworthy: "That man Theotocopulos is right. This thing mustn't be. It is human sacrifice. Maurice, my son!"

Cabal takes his arm.

Cabal: "There is still a month and more ahead of us. Let us talk it over calmly, Passworthy. There is a month yet. This is a shock to you. It was a shock for me. But perhaps it is less dreadful—and something greater—than you think. Consider it for a day or so. Let us all dine together—let us meet in three days' time, and tell each other plainly all that we have in our minds."

Cabal is shown in close-up with Passworthy: "I won't come back to the city with you. There is someone else to whom I must talk. I have to talk."

Passworthy: "No one is as closely interested as we are."

Cabal: "I don't know. She has a kind of claim. Many people would say it was as strong a claim as ours."

Passworthy: "And who is that?"

Cabal: "Catherine's mother. The woman who used to be my wife. . . . Didn't you know I had a wife? Or do you think Catherine came suddenly out of my head? Like Pallas Athene? I had a wife and she was very much a woman and we parted years ago."

Evening passes to twilight. After-sunset glow in the sky. A terrace with clipped yew trees (new type of yew) looking out over a wide landscape with the sea in the distance. Standing out against the sea is a huge heavy mortar-like structure. This is the Space Gun. It is our first sight of this. It crouches monstrously, dwarfing every other detail in the landscape. A certain mistiness enhances, if anything, its portentous dimensions.

An aeroplane sweeps down and its shadow passed across the terrace.

A momentary glimpse is given of Cabal descending from the plane he has flown to this place. Then the camera returns to the terrace to await him.

Cabal enters and walks slowly to the terrace balustrade. He stands musing, looking at the Space Gun. His hands are behind his back. So he remains for some moments.

He turns at a footfall and Rowena enters. Rowena is the descendant of Roxana, the favourite of the Boss of Everytown in 1970, just as Oswald Cabal is the descendant of John Cabal. She is physically like her prototype—the part is played by the same actress—but she has none of the arms-akimbo dash of her ancestress. She is better bred. She is dressed much more beautifully and with nothing of Roxana's sluttish magnificence, and her gestures are well under control.

Rowena: "And so at last I am permitted to see you again."

Cabal: "You heard the news quickly, Rowena."

Rowena: "It is all over the world now."

Cabal: "Already?"

Rowena: "On the air everywhere. The whole world talks of nothing else. Why have you done this thing to me? Our daughter!"

Cabal: "I did not do this to you. She determined to go. What do you want with me?"

Rowena: "You are a monster. You and your kind are monsters. Your science and your new orders have taken away your souls and put machines and theories in the place of them. It is well I left you when I did."

Cabal: "And you have come here—you have insisted on seeing me in order to tell me that—*now*."

Rowena: "Not only that. I forbid you to send our daughter on this mad expedition."

Cabal: "*Our* daughter! *My* daughter. You left her to me when you went away. And she goes—of her own free will."

Rowena: "Because you have poisoned her mind. She, I suppose, is one of the new sort of women just as you are one of the new sort of men. Do you think I do not care for her, simply because you have never let me see her?"

Cabal: "Usually you have been on the other side of the earth. Love-hunting."

Rowena: "Reproach me! All the same I care. Who left me love-hungry? . . . Cabal, have you no pity? Have you no imagination? If I cannot forbid—well, then I *implore*. Think of that body of hers—scarcely more than a child's body—crushed, broken, frozen!"

Cabal: "I won't. One can think too much of bodies, Rowena."

Rowena: "Hard you are and terrible. What are you doing with life, Cabal?"

Cabal: "Soft you are and sensuous. What are *you* doing with life?"

Rowena: "You turn it to steel."

Cabal: "You fritter it away."

Rowena: "Who made me fritter it away? I have been wanting to meet you face to face for years, and have this out with you. I hated leaving you. But you made life too high and hard for me."

Cabal: "I hated your going. But you made life too distracted and vexatious for me. I loved you—but loving you was an all-time task. I had work to do."

Rowena: "*What* work?"

Cabal: "The everlasting work of fighting danger and death and decay for mankind."

Rowena: "Fanatic! Where are danger and death to-day?"

Cabal: "In ambush everywhere."

H

Rowena: "You go out to meet them."

Cabal: "I had rather be the hunter than the hunted."

Rowena: "But if you are hunting danger and death all the time, what is there left of life?"

Cabal: "Courage, adventure, work—and an increasing power and greatness."

Rowena: "Give me love."

Cabal: "You left me for that. Poor love-huntress. My love wasn't good enough—not flattering enough—not sedulous enough. Have you ever found that love of your dreams? Was there ever a lover who made you feel as glorious as you wanted to be? Could any lover do that? Wherever you found love, you gripped it as a child plucks a flower—and you killed it."

Rowena: "Have I been anything but human?"

Cabal: "No."

Rowena: "I have loved after my nature. Even if at last I have to grow old and die."

Cabal: "But let me live after *my* nature. You may want love, but I want the stars."

Rowena: "But love too! You wanted human love once, Cabal."

Cabal: "I wanted my work more."

Rowena: "But isn't that girl of ours at least human? As I am? Isn't she entitled to the freshness of life—to the novelty of life? Is she to begin where you leave off? Suppose after all love *does* come to an end—gets found out? Why shouldn't she have her years of delusion and excitement?"

Cabal: "And end in futility? Left behind by all your loving? Painted? In an imitation of youth? Clinging to passion?"

Rowena: "Oh, you can sting. Which of the two is futility? To obey your impulses or deny them? That girl, I tell you, is a human being, and she has to follow the human way. She's a woman."

Cabal: "Not one of the old sort, Rowena. Not of your sort. Do you think that everything else in human life is going to alter, scale and power and speed, and men and women remain as they have always been? This is a New World we are living in. It drives to new and greater destinies. And that desperate old love story which has been acted and told so often, as though it was the very core of life, is almost finished with."

Rowena: "And you think *she* has finished with it?"

Cabal: "What do you know of our daughter? What do you know, you love-huntress, of the creative drive a woman can feel as well as a man? She has loved and she loves; she has found a mate and they are driving on together. Shoulder to shoulder. Almost forgetting each other in their happy identification. She lives for the endless adventure—as he lives for the endless adventure. And that is the increase of human knowledge and power—for ever. . . ."

Rowena: "Cabal, all men are fools about women. All of them. That girl of yours. And your endless adventure! You think she is a new sort of woman. There is no new sort of woman. She flies off—with her lover. Well, what sort of woman wouldn't—old sort or new sort? What could be more glorious?"

Cabal: "Anyhow she shall fly off."

Rowena: "The new sort of man seems to me to be very like the old sort of mule. Now tell me, tell me, if men are going to give themselves to this everlasting adventure of yours, what is to become of women?"

Cabal: "There's no sex in that sort of adventure. It is as open to you as it is to us. Drop the old sex romance. Come and work with us."

Rowena: "Work *with* you!"

Cabal: "Why not? You have hands and brains."

Rowena: "You mean, my dear, work *for* you. There speaks the old sort of man asking woman to be his slave. When it comes to women, is the new sort of man any different from the old?"

Cabal: "Why *for* us and not *with* us?"

Rowena: "Because you men have a way of taking the lead and getting hold of things."

Cabal: "Very well! *For* us if you like. And why not? Pick your man for the work he does, and the powers he has. Follow him and be his woman?"

Rowena: "We, we women, are to help and comfort and cherish—play the role of handmaid—to the end of things?"

Cabal: "If that's how you are made, and it seems to be how you are made; why not?"

Rowena: "It isn't how we are made."

Cabal: "If you are not made for knowledge and power as men are, if you are not made to serve knowledge and power, then what on earth *are* you made for? If you are more than a love-huntress, what do you dream you are hunting?"

Rowena: "Oh, we argued like this fifteen years ago?"

Cabal: "Fifteen years ago! This argument began before the Stone Age."

Rowena: "And it will end——! Will it ever end?"

Cabal: "Never for us, Rowena. Never—for generations yet. You go your way after your fashion—and I go mine."

Rowena: "And that is your last word for me—you who once knelt at my feet!"

Old memories come back to Cabal, a rush of forgotten emotions. He turns towards her. He seems full of things he cannot express and he says nothing.

Fade out of the two facing each other in the twilight,

man and woman, bereaved of all the illusion they ever had for one another and still—perplexed.

Cabal is in his brightly-lit office again. He still wears his out-of-doors cloak and he sits down with a certain weariness. He turns to the apparatus on his desk. "And now let us hear what Mr. Theotocopulos has to say about it all. This is the time for him."

He touches a button.

"I want to hear and see Theotocopulos. He must be talking now upon the mirrors everywhere."

Then the scene is changed to a great open space in which a big crowd has assembled before a gigantic screen at the head of a flight of stairs.

Theotocopulos is seen in the midst of a group of friends. He is no longer in his sculptor's overalls. He is dressed in an ornate, richly-embroidered, coloured satin costume, with a great cloak about him which he flourishes dramatically. He is ascending by the side of the gigantic screen in comparison with which he and his party are quite minute. They glance at the crowd and their voices are lost in the general babble. They pass behind the gigantic mirror and then suddenly Theotocopulos appears in the mirror, vastly magnified, and his voice dominates all other sounds.

The crowd of small figures sways with excitement as he prepares to begin.

Then the picture goes back to Cabal sitting in his study and preparing to listen to the discourse of Theotocopulos. The room is silent. Then a confused sound like the sound of a crowd is heard and the televisor disk becomes cloudy. Cabal makes an adjustment and the sounds and the picture become clear together.

The televisor disk advances so as to occupy the great area of the screen. It is framed below by Cabal's head and shoulders.

"What is all this Progress? What is the good of this Progress? Onward and onward. We demand a halt, we demand a rest. The object of life is happy living. . . ."

Cabal: "One would think the object of life was everlasting repetition."

"We will not have life sacrificed to experiment. Progress is not living, it should only be the preparation for living."

Cabal stands up, walks a few paces away from the disk, and turns to hear more.

"Let us be just to these people who rule over us. Let us not be ungrateful. They have tidied up the world. They have tidied it up marvellously. Order and magnificence is achieved, knowledge increases. Oh God, how it increases!" (Laughter.)

Cabal grimly: "So they laugh at that."

"Still the hard drive goes on. They find work for all of us. We thought this was to be the Age of Leisure. But is it? We must measure and compute, we must collect and sort and count. We must sacrifice ourselves. We must live for— what is it?—the species. We must sacrifice ourselves all day and every day to this incessant spreading of knowledge and order. We gain the whole world—and at what a price! Greater sacrifices and still greater. And at last they lead us back to the supreme sacrifice—the sacrifice of human life. They stage the old Greek tragedy again and a father offers up his daughter to his evil gods."

With an impatient movement Cabal extinguishes the televisor. "And that voice is sounding over all the world. I wonder what the world is making of it."

He faces his apartment.

"We might suppress it.

"Make an end of free expression. That would be the beginning of the end of progress.

"No. They have to hear him, and make what they can of him. But I wish I could be all over the world now, listening with every listener. What will they make of him?"

PART XIII

World Audience

THIS is a sequence of scenes and passing shots to portray the enormous range and the simultaneousness of thought and discussion in the new world. The discourse of Theotocopulos goes on almost uninterruptedly except for occasional shouts and outcries, until at last he comes to his end. He appears in different mirrors and in different frames and at times he is heard and not seen. But the reality of a single person being able to speak to the whole world, so far as it is interested and will listen, and the swiftness with which a common response can be evoked at the same time in every part of the earth where listeners can be found, is made plain.

We see first of all the backs of a considerable number of people who are dining together. They give a glimpse of the fashions of 2055, and the tableware of an eating place. They look up at a large frame in which Theotocopulos is seen and heard talking. The crowd is attentive, but displays little reaction to his speech. Then the flash passes to the edge of a swimming pool or to the border of a lawn on which a number of young people in athletic clothing applaud a wrestler who has just put down an antagonist. A man stands up and switches on a televisor and everybody listens. Some of them mutter comments to each other and opinion is divided.

Then one passes to a number of scientific people working in a laboratory. Theotocopulos is seen talking on the televisor. One man is irritated and says: "Oh, stop his nonsense." Theotocopulos is switched off. Then an Oriental young woman with a fan, reclining indolently on a couch under a window that looks out upon palms, listens gravely to an oval televisor on which Theotocopulos continues his speech. Then there is a mountain hut with a glass window giving upon a violent snowstorm. Two workers in arctic costume occupy the hut; one lies on a bed; the other sits at a table and listens to the voice. They switch it off. "I suppose that rubbish appeals to the crowds in the town. What do they know of real work?"

A group of modellers is seen in a studio. It is large, but not fundamentally different from an art studio of to-day. There have been no great changes in the plastic arts. In the background is the televisor. An artist is focusing this and Theotocopulos becomes visible and audible. . . .

First Modeller: "Hear! Hear!"

Second Modeller: "No! No!"

He turns the televisor off. "A man has a right to do what he likes with himself."

First Modeller: "Never. That Space Gun ought to be destroyed. And now!"

Third Modeller: "The things ought to stop. Look!" He takes up a model.

All: "Good for Theotocopulos."

Fourth Modeller: "But here!" He holds up an ugly caricature of Cabal. (Laughter.)

This is the discourse of Theotocopulos which is distributed over these scenes.

"These people who are so kind as to manage our world for us declare that they leave us free to do as we please, they assert in season and out of season that never has there been such freedom as we have to-day. And as the price of this limitless freedom we enjoy, they ask us to ignore the hard and dreadful persistence of their own inhuman researches. But is our freedom really the freedom they pretend it is? Is a man free who cannot protest at what he sees and hears? We want the freedom to arrest. We want the freedom to prevent. Have they the right to use the resources of this world to torment us by the spectacle of their cruel and mad adventures? Have they the right to mar the very peace of our starry heavens by human sacrifices?

"In the old days, as we all know, there lay deep dark shadows on the happiness of men, and these shadows were called religions. You have heard of them. Puritanism and the mortification of the flesh, shaven heads and cropped spirits. *Thou shalt* and *Thou shalt not*, oppressing the free hearts of men. You have learnt about these tyrannies of the spirit in your histories. Those old religions were bad enough with their sacrifices and vows—their horrible celibacy, their gloomy chantings, their persecutions and inquisitions. We thought we were free of religions for ever. But have they really left us—or have they merely adopted new names and fresh masks? I tell you this science and exploration of theirs is no more and no less than the spirit of self-immolation returning to the earth in a new disguise. No more and no less. It is the old black spirit of human subjugation, Jove, the pitiless monster, coming back in the midst of our freedom and abundance—the old dark seriousness—the stern unnecessary devotions. What has brought it back? Why have we all this insistence on duty and sacrifice for the young, on discipline, self-restraint and strain now? What is the need for it now? What does it mean? What does it portend? Make no mistake about it! The servitudes they put upon themselves to-day they will impose upon the whole world to-morrow. Is man *never* to rest, never to be free? A time will come when they will want more cannon fodder for their Space Guns—when you in your turn will be forced away to take your chance upon strange planets and in dreary and abominable places beyond the friendly stars. I tell you we must stop this insensate straining towards strange and inhuman experiences—and we must stop it now. I say: an end to this Progress. Make an end to Progress now. We are content with the simple sensuous, limited, lovable life of man and we want no other. Between the dark past of history and the incalculable future let us snatch to-day—and *live*. What is the future to us? Give the earth peace and leave our human lives alone."

A phosphorescent drusy cavity deep in the earth. A drusy cavity is a cavity in a rock into which minerals have been free to crystallise for immemorial ages. There are big dark and light crystals in crowded confusion. Into this the nose of a borer pierces its way laterally and comes to a stop. It withdraws and two young men and a girl, in shiny, white, close-fitting clothes with glow lamps on their foreheads, creep into the cavernous space.

First Young Man: "Here we are ten miles below the surface. And no molten rock but instead this Aladdin's cave."

The Girl: "And precious stones! What wouldn't my great-grandmother have given for them!"

Second Young Man: "I wonder what is going on up above."

He is carrying a small televisor on his chest in the position of a breast-pocket and he swings it into position to look at it.

The others look also over his shoulder. The televisor shows Theotocopulos bowing and turning away. Sound effect: a rush of applause.

The Girl: "It's Theotocopulos. He's finished. But we know what he had to say. We have heard it all before. Is there anything else?"

First Young Man: "This Theotocopulos is an old imbecile."

Second Young Man: "The dear little children are not to take risks any more for ever. Just play with their little painties and sing their little songs."

First Young Man: "And find out nice new peculiar ways of making lovey-povey."

Second Young Man: "But mind, you, that stuff is going to stir up a lot of the lazy people in the towns. They *hate* this endless exploration and experimenting. What business is it of theirs? It's a sort of envy they feel. It wounds their pride. They do not want to do this work themselves, but they cannot suffer anyone else to do it. . . ."

The scene changes to the crowd which has assembled before the great central screen behind which Theotocopulos has been talking. The crowd is dispersing, and we see their faces.

One man says to another: "He's right. The Space Gun is an offence to every human instinct."

A Woman: "If I was that man Passworthy I would *kill* Cabal."

A Man: "It makes me long for the good old days when there was honest warfare and simple devotion to honour and the flag. Space Guns indeed! What is the world coming to?"

The Woman: "I wish *I'd* lived in the good old days before all this horrible science took possession of us."

Three very old men sit in a pretty vine-covered arbour drinking and talking. They are hale and hearty. They might well be lean good-looking old gentlemen of sixty. Like all the people of the new age, their abundant hair is trim and neat—but artificially silvered.

First Old Man: "To-day is my birthday."

Second Old Man: "And how much is that?"

First Old Man: "A hundred and two."

Second Old Man: "I'm only ninety-eight."

Third Old Man: "But I score a hundred and nine."

First Old Man: "Where should we have been a century ago?"

Second Old Man: "Under the earth."

First Old Man: "Or worse."

Third Old Man breaks into song: "Oh your glasses raise to the good old days."

Chorus: *"Gout and rheumatics and toothless jaws."*

Solo : " That are gone for ever, to God be praise.

    The dark and the haste and the dirty ways.

    Diabetes and body rot

    Deafness and blindness, the pitiful lot."

Chorus: *"Gout and rheumatics and toothless jaws."*

Third Old Man: "Of ancient men in the good old days."

They drink to each other.

First Old Man, after an appreciative pause: "And that's one for Theotocopulos."

A nursery of children. Anno 2055. They play with plasticine, draw on sheets of paper (as they do at Dartington), build with bricks or run about after each other. There may be a Siamese or white Persian kitten in the party or tame red squirrels scampering about.

Two women in the foreground converse.

First Woman: "In 1900 one infant in every six died in the first year. Now it is the rarest thing in the world for an infant to die."

Second Woman: "*Was* it one in six?"

First Woman: "That was the best in all the world. That was the English rate. And out of every hundred women who bore children, three were doomed to die. Think of it: Thousands of them every year. Death in childbirth is now a thing unheard of. But that was the natural way of life."

A very great scientific laboratory in the year 2055. It is in tier above tier in a huge space, so that there are hundreds of workers, men and women, mostly clad in white overalls, visible. Scientific work has become multitudinous. They work at benches and tables. At certain points there are vivid splutterings of light. In the foreground two men are watching some brightly illuminated globes and tanks in which small fish-like creatures are seen moving, not very distinctly.

Their attention is called to something off the screen and there enters a woman carrying a very intelligent-looking little dog.

First Scientific Worker: "Hullo! What have you got there?"

The Woman: "This is the last word in Canine Genetics. Pavlov started this work in Russia, six score years ago. Look at this little dear. It can almost talk. It will never have distemper. It will live to be thirty, good and strong. And it runs like the wind. Wag your tail, my darling, and thank Uncle Science for your blessings."

Somebody shouts to the other workers: "The Dog up to date. Come and look."

Workers on various of the tiers leave their benches and come down to see. Others intent on their work disregard the excitement. A little crowd assembles about the new specimen.

Second Scientific Worker: "We must teach him to bite Theotocopulos."

Third Scientific Worker, with disgust: "Oh! Theotocopulos!"

The Woman: "The dear old world! I suppose you and I would have been working in a slum for fourpence an hour. Instead of being friends with the very best little dog in the world." Petting. "Ain't it? Yess."

Crowd about the dog.

First Scientific Worker: "Most of us would hardly have learnt to read—and we should have been clerks and drudges."

Second Scientific Worker: "Or out-of-works."

The Woman: "And now there is always something new and something exciting. Oh! save me from that natural life of man."

First Scientific Worker: "What *is* the natural life of man?"

Second Scientific Worker: "Lice and fleas. Endless infections. Croup to begin with and cancer to finish. Rotten teeth by forty. Anger and spite. . . . And yet these fools listen to Theotocopulos. They want Romance! They want flags back. War and all the nice *human* things. They think we are Robots—and that drilled soldiers in the old days weren't. They want the Dear Old World of the Past—and an end to all this wicked Science! . . ."

PART XIV

The Struggle for the Space Gun

THE scene is an ante-room to the dining alcove where Cabal, Passworthy, Catherine and Maurice are to dine. They dine at half-past four or five, for dinner has got back to the hours it had in the seventeenth century and lunch has disappeared. People breakfast, dine and sup, and there is a great variety about the meal hours, because there is no twenty-four hour alternation now of light and darkness.

The alcove is a sort of glazed balcony projecting over one of the great City Ways. When the glass is closed, it is quite silent. When it is opened sounds come up from below. On a couch Maurice and Catherine sit close together, and very content with each other. They look up as if through the transparent ceiling at something in the air and then stand up as Passworthy appears through a small door that leads from above.

Passworthy: "And so we've had our three days for reflection. Haven't you two thought better of it?"

Maurice: "We couldn't think better of it, Father. Don't make things hard for us."

Passworthy to Catherine: "Where is *your* father?"

Catherine: "He was coming here with me, but he had a call from Morden Mitani, who had something urgent to say to him."

Passworthy: "Morden Mitani?"

Catherine: "The Controller of Traffic and Order. My father waited behind to talk to him."

Cabal's apartment. Cabal is greeting Morden Mitani, who is an efficient good-looking man in a dark costume. Cabal says: "I was starting out to dine in the Cupola buildings. I am already overdue."

Morden Mitani: "Then I won't keep you here talking. I will come with you towards the Cupola through the City Ways. It will be best like that. There are things I want you to see and know about."

One of the City Ways. Morden Mitani and Cabal walk across the scene and arrive at a vantage point on a high bridge looking down over a great arena far below.

Mitani: "That is what I want you to see."

Far below a little straggle of people is gathering into a sort of procession. Camera shot at them from high above. They are singing a song of revolt.

Cabal: "What are they doing? Is it some procession? It straggles a lot."

Mitani: "That's—what do they call it? A demonstration. Trouble."

Cabal: "But what's the trouble?"

Mitani draws him back behind a pilaster. Other people come to the bridge in order to see the crowd below. They do not observe Cabal and Mitani.

Confidential close up of Cabal and Mitani.

Mitani (in a low tone): "That is the outcome of Theotocopulos. He ought never to have been allowed to talk on the mirrors."

Cabal: "The world must have free speech. We can't go back on that. People must think for themselves."

Mitani: "Then the world will have to have policeman again. Just to keep people from acting too quickly on a chance suggestion."

Cabal: "What can he do?"

Mitani: "People are taking him very seriously. They are taking him *very* seriously. They want to stop the firing of the Space Gun by force. They talk of—how do they put it?— *rescuing the victims*."

Cabal: "But what is this? If the victims choose to go?"

Mitani: "Still they object."

Cabal: "And if they object?"

Mitani: "They will interfere with things. They are making —what did they use to call it?—an insurrection. That down there is insurrection."

Cabal: "Against whom?"

Mitani: "Against the Council."

Cabal: "An insurrection! I cannot imagine it. In the past insurrections were risings of downtrodden classes—and now we have no downtrodden classes. Everyone does a share in the work and everyone has a share in the abundance. Can mankind rise against itself? No. *That* down there is just —a little excitement. What can Theotocopulos do with it?"

Mitani: "He gathers large crowds. That sort of thing is going on all over the city. We have no police, no troops, no weapons nowadays to keep crowds in order. We thought that was done with for ever. 'Rescue the victims from Cabal,' he says. He keeps on against you. 'Rescue the victims from Cabal.'"

Cabal: "Isn't one of them my daughter?—My only daughter."

Mitani: "He says that merely shows your hardness of heart—shows what a monster science may make out of a man. He compares you with those Greek parents who sent their children to the Minotaur."

Cabal: "And if I sent other people's children and saved my own?"

Mitani: "You'd be in the wrong with him anyway."

I

Cabal: "But after all—what can he do?"

Mitani: "There is the Space Gun out on the seashore. It is hardly guarded at all. Nothing has been guarded on this planet for the past fifty years."

Cabal: "Then you'll have to organise some sort of guard. After all you have your way-men and your inspection planes. That ought to be enough. And if there is much disturbance—isn't there still the Gas of Peace?"

Mitani: "There *is* none."

Cabal: "*Is* there none?"

Mitani: "Officially anyhow. There has been no need of it. The world has been orderly because it has been happy, and it has been happy because everyone has had something to do. There has been no reason to keep any of that gas. There has been no use for it for seventy years. But now I want to call up the Council and get a sanction to make it at once—and use it if need be."

Cabal: "Call the Council, but won't that take too long?"

Mitani: "Well, I have been anticipating a little. I have been having some made."

Cabal: "That is right. We can endorse that."

Mitani: "In a few hours some tons at any rate will be ready and our planes will be ready to distribute it. But still —it will take a little time. Some hours, perhaps."

Cabal: "That old Gas of Peace. We shall hate to use it again. But if the people will not give us the freedom of outer space—we shall have to use it."

Mitani: "I have your support then in what I am doing?"

Cabal: "Fully. Yet all this is incredible to me. Insurrection! Against exploration! Mankind turning upon science and adventure. Wanting to call a halt. It's a mood, Mitani."

Mitani: "It is a dangerous mood."

Cabal: "It's a fit of nerves—at the thought of stepping

off this planet and leaping into space. Well—first we must save the gun."

Mitani: "That first."

Mitani goes and Cabal approaches the screen.

Cabal in soliloquy: "Have we been making the pace too hard for Humanity? Humanity! What *is* Humanity? Is it Theotocopulos? Is it dear old Passworthy? Is it Rowena? Is it I?"

The dining alcove. Far below, the streets are seen. The meal is nearly finished. Cabal, Passworthy, Catherine and Maurice. Maurice touches a button, and a plate with fruits arrives on a glassy band. Maurice puts the plate on the table. Catherine and he begin to eat. Passworthy does not eat. He looks at the young people. Presently he speaks.

Passworthy: "Isn't life good enough for you here? Here you are in a safe and lovely world. Young lovers. Just beginning life. And you want to go into that outer horror! Let someone go who is sick of life."

Catherine: "They want fit young people, alert and quick. And we are fit young people. We can observe, we can come back and tell."

Passworthy: "Cabal! I want to ask you one plain question. Why do you let your daughter dream of going on this mad moon journey?"

Cabal was sitting silently in thought. Now he looks at his daughter and answers slowly: "Because I love her. Because I want her to live to the best effect. Dragging out life to the last possible second isn't living to the best effect. The nearer the bone, the sweeter the meat. The best of life, Passworthy, lies nearest to the edge of death."

Catherine stretches out her hand to him. Cabal takes Catherine's hand.

Passworthy: "I am a broken man. I do not know where honour lies."

Cabal to his daughter: "My dear, I love you—and I have no doubt."

Maurice: "A century ago, no man who was worth his salt hesitated to give his life in war. When I read about those fellows in the trenches——"

Cabal: "No. Only a few men *gave* their lives in war. Those few men were caught in some tragic and noble necessity. What the rest did was to *risk* their lives—and that is all you two have to do. You two have to do your utmost to come back safe and sound. And you are not the only ones who are taking risks to-day. Have we not men exploring the depths of the sea, training and making friends with dangerous animals and with danger in every shape and form, playing with gigantic physical forces, balancing on the rims of lakes of molten metal——"

Passworthy: "But all that is to make the world safe for Man—safe for happiness."

Cabal: "No. The world will never be safe for man—and there is no happiness in safety. You haven't got things right, Passworthy. Our fathers and our fathers' fathers cleaned up the old order of things because it killed children, because it killed people unprepared for death, because it tormented people in vain, because it outraged human pride and dignity, because it was an ugly spectacle of waste. But that was only the beginning. There is nothing wrong in suffering, if you suffer for a purpose. Our revolution did not abolish death or danger. It simply made death and danger worth while."

Morden Mitani enters suddenly. He is in a state of intense excitement. Cabal stands up abruptly with an anxious face.

Mitani: "Cabal! The gun is in urgent danger. It is a race against time now to save it. Things have happened very rapidly. Theotocopulos is out with a crowd of people already. He is going to the Space Gun now. They are going to break it up. They say it is the symbol of your tyranny."

Cabal: "Have they weapons?"

Mitani: "Bars of metal. They can smash electric cables. They can do no end of mischief."

Cabal: "Are there no weapons on our side? Cannot your traffic control produce a police?"

Mitani: "Very few. . . . We have nothing but the Gas of Peace. And it isn't ready. It will take hours yet. There are some young people we can gather. We must hold this crowd back—at any cost—for a time; until the Gas of Peace can be brought up."

Passworthy, at a window: "Look!"

Cabal and the rest come to the window. Passworthy points to the streets far below. He opens the window. Sudden sound effects. Camera follows his eyes from above. Crowd marching and singing their song of revolt. Cabal and his party looking down.

A technical assistant hurries in and goes up to Mitani. He speaks but is inaudible. Cabal makes gesture to the window, which Mitani closes. Noise cut off.

Assistant: "It is a riot. It is barbarism come back."

Cabal: "Who are you?"

Assistant shows the identification disk on his gauntlet. Disk with inscription: "William Jeans. Astronomical Staff— Space Gun."

Mitani: "*They* must go afoot. We have stopped the air ways. They will take an hour or more to get there. Even those who have started already. And *then* they will hesitate."

Assistant: "That gun must not be broken up. That vast

piece of work. The pity of it!—if they smash it! When the trial experiments have all been made! When everything was ready!"

Maurice: "When everything was ready." He is struck by a thought; he looks at Catherine. Catherine understands him.

Passworthy: "And if they smash up this infernal gun— then honour is satisfied and you need not go."

Maurice: "Oh, Father! Father!"

Cabal: "They won't smash the gun."

Maurice, eagerly to assistant: "Suppose the gun was fired now? Would the cylinder reach the moon?"

Assistant, looking at his watch: "It would miss now and fly into outer space. But . . . it is now five. If the gun is fired about seven. . . ."

Catherine: "And . . . it *could* be?"

Assistant: "Yes."

Maurice and Catherine look at each other. They understand each other.

Catherine: "Then . . ."

Maurice: "We go now."

Cabal: "And why not?"

Assistant: "That is perfectly possible."

Passworthy cries out: "I protest! . . . Oh! I don't know what to say. Don't go. Don't go."

Maurice: "If we don't go now—we may never go. And all the rest of our lives we shall feel that we have shirked, and lived in vain. . . . This supremely is what we two are for. . . . Father, we have to go."

A tunnel leading out of the city. Effect of mob marching to the gun. Effect of mob coming out of tunnel.

Mob groups from different city entrances collecting together and marching to the gun. (This mob, by the by, is as well dressed as any other people in the film. It has the well-groomed look which is universal in the new world. It is not a social conflict we are witnessing. It is not the Haves attacked by the Have-Nots; it is the Doers attacked by the Do-Nots.)

PART XV

The Firing of the Space Gun

IN an aeroplane. Cabal, Passworthy, Catherine and Maurice. They are flying to the gun. They look out of the windows. The gun is seen in the distance like a great metallic beast brooding among the hills.

Through the windows we see next that the plane is descending *vertically* close to the Space Gun. First clouds, then cliff, and then through great girders, cables and machinery. The plane comes to rest close to the colossal shock absorbers of the gun.

Mitani meets Cabal, Passworthy, Catherine and Maurice as they are getting out of the aeroplane, and they look upwards at the gun. The camera reveals the massive proportions of this structure.

The Space Gun, monumental, tremendous, overwhelming. On the framework are young athletes who discover Catherine and Maurice and hail them enthusiastically. Catherine and Maurice go towards their friends. Fraternal reception. Cabal, Passworthy and Mitani follow slowly.

They come to a lift. Cabal and Passworthy stand at the entrance. Mitani is beside the door.

Mitani to Cabal: "Go up to the platform. We can guard this below."

Cabal and Passworthy enter the lift.

The lift arrives on a high platform a score of yards or so below the level of the cylinder which is to be shot at the moon. This hangs at present over the mouth of the gun, and is held by almost invisibly delicate metal supports.

Cabal comes out from the lift upon this high platform, followed by Passworthy. Cabal goes to a railing and looks down. Camera follows Cabal's eyes and shows the Space Gun from above. In the distance are Theotocopulos and his crowd advancing through the supports towards the Space Gun. Cabal, Passworthy, Catherine, and Maurice stand on platform. They look up. The cylinder is seen close above their heads being lowered slowly towards the muzzle of the gun.

The insurrectionary song increases in volume as it draws nearer.

Theotocopulos and his mob appear. They appear at the edge of the cliff, they come up against the sky and no difficulties in production must be allowed to minimise the dramatic effect of their appearance upon the cliff edge.

They stop abruptly—(the song stops also)—and they stare. Shots of Theotocopulos and his crowd staring upward.

The cylinder being lowered until it hangs at the mouth of the gun.

Theotocopulos discovers Cabal and points: "There is the man——"

Cries of indignation.

Camera passes slowly over to Cabal across the framework and structures about the gun, giving the impression of a great gulf between the two men. The subsequent conversation is shouted by means of amplifiers across a great space. These amplifiers must be indicated, but not obtrusively.

Behind Cabal are Passworthy, Catherine and Maurice. A young mechanic approaches them.

Mechanic: "Everything is ready."

There is a moment of tension.

Catherine takes a quite silent leave of her father. Maurice grips Passworthy's hands in both of his in an attempt to reassure him and give him courage and dignity.

Catherine and Maurice turn away, followed by the mechanic. A close-up of Cabal shows his face distressfully calm.

Theotocopulos (off): "There is the man who would offer up his daughter to the Devil of Science."

Cabal becomes aware of these words, and is roused by them; he walks to the railing and addresses Theotocopulos: "What do you want here?"

The picture now passes to Theotocopulos and remains with him during the subsequent talk. Cabal is heard but not seen.

Theotocopulos: "We want to save these young people from your experiments. We want to put an end to this inhuman foolery. We want to make the world safe for men. We mean to destroy that gun."

Cabal: "And how will you do that?"

Theotocopulos: "Oh! we have electricians with *us* too."

Cabal: "We have a right to do what we like with our own lives—with our sort of lives."

Theotocopulos: "How can we do that when your science and inventions are perpetually changing life for us—when you are everlastingly rebuilding and contriving strange things about us? When you make what we think great seem small. When you make what we think strong seem feeble.

We don't want you in the same world with us. We don't want this expedition. We don't want mankind to go out to the moon and the planets. We shall hate you more if you succeed than if you fail. Is there never to be rest in this world?"

The picture returns to Passworthy and Cabal on the platform.

Passworthy has listened to the dialogue suffering mutely. Now he turns upon Cabal. But he shouts for everyone to hear.

Passworthy: "Yes, I too, ask you, is there never to be rest? Never? This is my son. And he has rebelled against me. What he does, he does against the instincts of my heart. Cabal, I implore you. Is there never to be calm and happiness for mankind?"

A tremendous outburst greets his words from the mob. The picture passes to the crowd. They begin to move by a common impulse towards the Space Gun. We see them first as a flash of faces and then from very far off. They are seen then like a streaming multitude of ants pouring across the floor of a big room.

The top of the Gun with the cylinder in its muzzle. Catherine and Maurice stand by a screw door, which resembles the window of a liner's port-hole, in the bottom of the cylinder. They have special clothes on now, very simple, and close to the body. They are assisted by mechanics to take their places within the cylinder.

Flash back to the crowd scrambling down lattices from the cliff edge towards the Gun.

Inside the cylinder which is lit from below. Catherine and Maurice, hanging to their handfasts, spread eagle fashion. The faces of the mechanics are seen below. Maurice looks at Catherine.

Maurice: "Do you want to go back?"

Catherine smiles: "Hold firm, my dear."

The door of the cylinder is screwed in slowly—gradually the scene becomes dark, until it is quite dark, and the faces and figures of Catherine and Maurice are lost in the darkness.

The crowd is seen swarming upon the framework over against the gun.

On the platform, Mitani looks down at the crowd and then at his wrist watch. He looks up at the cylinder.

The cylinder from below. It is very slowly lowered and it disappears entirely into the gun. Its supports are detached and retire.

The crowd is seen clambering amidst the framework at the base of the gun.

Cabal is seen standing alone. He is moved by his own thoughts and feelings to speech. He comes to the railing: "Listen, Theotocopulos! If I wished to give way to you, I could not. It is not we who war against the order of things, but you. Either life goes forward or it goes back. That is the law of life."

Theotocopulos dismisses the argument by a gesture: "We will destroy the gun."

His following shout agreement and resume their scattered unplanned advance.

Cabal and Passworthy are seen on the platform and in the background stands a mechanic in front of the small heavy open door of a concussion chamber. Cabal leans over a railing watching the crowd below.

Cabal (shouting down): "Before you can even reach the base of the gun, it will be fired. Beware of the concussion."

He turns back. Passworthy motionless. Cabal pulls Passworthy towards the heavy door.

The mob is seen on the ground swarming about the gun supports. People, many of whom carry heavy metallic bars, are attempting to injure the big metallic masses.

A table in an observation chamber. A hand rests by a button, waiting. There is a clock dial with a long delicate seconds hand.

Cabal's voice: "Beware!"

"Beware of the concussion."

The crowd hesitates. The noise of a heavy iron door as it clangs shut. A silence of expectation. The crowd realises it is too late. It wavers and then turns and begins to clamber down through the lattices into which it has struggled, and to run away in the spaces below the gun.

The table and the hand in the observation chamber. The seconds hand of the clock dial moves towards a marked point. As it does so the finger extends and presses a button.

Thud.

Large scale effects of concussion. Gun recoiling. Whirlwind sweeping the crowd.

Theotocopulos, standing out against the sky on a great metal girder, is caught in the whirlwind, and his cloak is blown over his head. He is left struggling ridiculously in his own cloak, and that is the last that is seen of him.

Clouds of dust obscure the screen and clear to show the crowd after the shock. Some press their ears as if they were painful, others stare under their hands up into the sky.

Then the crowd begins to stream back towards the city. Shots of them re-entering the city, in a straggling aimless manner, and pausing ever and again to stare at the sky.

PART XVI

Finale

Aₙ observatory at a high point above Everytown. A telescopic mirror of the night sky showing the cylinder as a very small speck against a starry background. Cabal and Passworthy stand before this mirror.

Cabal: "There! There they go! That faint gleam of light."
Pause.

Passworthy: "I feel—what we have done is—monstrous."

Cabal: "What they have done is magnificent."

Passworthy: "Will they return?"

Cabal: "Yes. And go again. And again— *until* the landing can be made and the moon is conquered. This is only a beginning."

Passworthy: "And if they don't return—my son, and your daughter? What of that, Cabal?"

Cabal (with a catch in his voice but resolute): "Then presently—others will go."

Passworthy: "My God! Is there never to be an age of happiness? Is there never to be rest?"

Cabal: "Rest enough for the individual man. Too much of it and too soon, and we call it death. But for MAN no rest and no ending. He must go on—conquest beyond conquest. This little planet and its winds and ways, and all the laws of mind and matter that restrain him. Then the planets about him, and at last out across immensity to the stars. And when he has conquered all the deeps of space and all the mysteries of time—still he will be beginning."

Passworthy: "But we are such little creatures. Poor humanity. So fragile—so weak."

Cabal: "Little animals, eh?"

Passworthy: "Little animals."

Cabal: "If we are no more than animals—we must snatch at our little scraps of happiness and live and suffer and pass, mattering no more—than all the other animals do—or have done." (He points out at the stars). "It is that—or this? All the universe—or nothingness. . . . Which shall it be, Passworthy?"

The two men fade out against the starry background until only the stars remain.

The musical finale becomes dominant.

Cabal's voice is heard repeating through the music: "Which shall it be, Passworthy? Which shall it be?"

A louder, stronger voice reverberates through the auditorium: "WHICH SHALL IT BE?"

THE END